The Newspaper Kids 3

Pegleg Paddy's Puppy Factory

First published in Australia by **Angus&Robertson** in 1996
An imprint of HarperCollins*Publishers*, Australia
First published in Great Britain by Collins 1999
Collins is an imprint of HarperCollins*Publishers* Ltd,
77-85 Fulham Palace Road, Hammersmith, London W6 8JB

The HarperCollins website address is www.**fireandwater**.com

3 5 7 9 8 6 4 2

Text copyright © Juanita Phillips 1996

ISBN 0 00 675462 7

The author asserts the moral right to be identified as author of the work

Printed and bound in Great Britain by
Omnia Books Limited, Glasgow

The Newspaper Kids 3

NEWSPAPER OFFICE

Pegleg Paddy's Puppy Factory

Juanita Phillips

Illustrations by Mark David

Collins

An Imprint of HarperCollins*Publishers*

Meet The Newspaper *Kids*

Hugo

Jasper and I are so close in age we are almost twins but, unlike me, my older sister can be a pain — she's always grabbing the good things for herself. So when it came to giving ourselves jobs on our newspaper, no one was more surprised than me to be given the job of chief reporter.

Chasing criminals and solving mysteries was what I'd always wanted to do, but chief reporter? That sounded important . . . and, what's even better, fun!

Jasper

Thank goodness, Hugo agreed to be chief reporter because while he's chasing criminals, someone has to interview the famous people . . . and that leaves me! It won't be easy — being glamorous is hard work. Most importantly, the kids of Blue Rock need a voice and mine's the loudest.

Everyone has a right to be heard; especially kids, and especially me!

Frankie

A reporter could have the best story in Blue Rock, an exclusive, but without a picture, the reporter has no proof. Luckily my nose for trouble and my eye for detail leads me and my cameras to be in the right place at the right time and SNAP! Instant evidence.

A picture speaks a thousand words, as my dad used to say, so when someone says — get the picture? I do!

Toby

Putting together a newspaper is a bit like putting together a jigsaw. And to put together a good newspaper, you need a lot of pieces.

That's why I am lucky to have Frankie's photographs and reporters like my best friend Jasper, and her brother, Hugo. What Jasper doesn't know, Hugo is sure to find out!

If a story breaks . . . the newspaper kids are on the case!

*For Mum and Dad, who taught me that the greatest joy
in life is a good book and a cubby-house to read it in ~ J. P.*

Chapter One

Dear Doctor Death,

I have a problem. Every morning at about 8.30 – just before I go to school – I get this really bad pain in my tummy. It's so bad I go cross-eyed and start going a bit mental. Before too long I'm barking like a dog and running around in circles. I've also noticed a huge lump growing on my shoulder. I think it's another head. I don't know what's wrong with me.

Please help!

Signed, Desperate.

PS This never happens during the holidays.

I finished typing and stared thoughtfully at the computer screen. Hmm. This was a tough one. It was a good thing Dr Death knew the answer.

> *Dear Desperate,*
>
> *Your problem is really very simple — you are allergic to school. This condition can be life-threatening if it is not treated. The second head you are growing is a result of over-exposure to teachers. They are much more toxic than nuclear radiation and, over time, can cause hideous deformities. Unfortunately, not many parents realise this. You must alert them before it is too late. Your life is clearly in danger and the only thing that can save you is a day off school.*

I chortled softly. We hadn't received any genuine letters for this month's Dr Death column, so Toby, the editor of our newspaper *Street Wise*, had assigned me to the job. At this rate I'd get it finished well before the deadline.

I moved on to the next problem.

> *Dear Doctor Death,*
>
> *While looking through my telescope one night, I noticed a giant asteroid hurtling*

*towards Earth at a million miles an hour.
It looks quite similar to the one that wiped
out the dinosaurs. By my calculations it will
hit Blue Rock within the next twenty-four
hours. Will this have any bad effects on
my health?*

Signed, Worried.

A heavy hand fell on my shoulder. I looked up. Yikes! It was Mr Bishop. I was so engrossed in Dr Death, I'd almost forgotten I was still at school.

'How's that essay going, Hugo? Almost finished?'

I quickly saved Dr Death to my private files so Mr Bishop couldn't see it.

'Nearly, sir. I just . . . ah . . . pushed the wrong button on the computer and lost it all. I guess I'll have to start again.'

My best friend Frankie kicked me under the desk. I could hear her trying not to laugh. Mr Bishop looked at his watch.

'Well, it's too late now. School's nearly finished for the day, and then it's . . .'

The bell rang, finishing his sentence for him.

'HOLIDAYS! Hooray!'

The class erupted into pandemonium. Yelling and cheering, we piled out of the classroom. I slipped the computer disk into my school bag and shot out the door after Frankie, adding my voice to the chorus of farewells.

'See you, Mr Bishop! Bye, Mr Bishop! Have a good holiday, sir!'

Funny, but I could have sworn Mr Bishop looked almost as happy as we were!

'Two whole weeks!' I kicked a stone and watched it skip up Tumblegum Street towards home. 'That's plenty of time to find a front page story.'

As chief reporter for our kids' newspaper, *Street Wise*, that's my job — breaking the big stories. In a small town like Blue Rock, where nothing much ever happens, it's not easy. But I've learned from experience that a good reporter can sniff out a story anywhere. You just have to keep your nose in the air, and your eyes and ears open. Like a dog. That's why they call us reporters newshounds!

'I'm going to start taking some photos tomorrow,' announced Frankie. 'Denis Wong's birthday party will be good for the social pages. He's having a magician.'

My sister Jasper got to the stone and gave it another kick. 'Well, I don't have a clue what story I'm going to do. I just hope Toby has some ideas.'

Jasper's the celebrity reporter. That's also a pretty tough job to have in Blue Rock. We don't get too many celebrities. Not that you'd ever say that to Jasper. 'You don't have to be famous to be a celebrity, just interesting,' she'd snap, with a flick of her long orange plaits. 'Besides, once I put them in *Street Wise*, they *are* famous.'

I was thinking so hard about the newspaper that I almost tripped over something. I looked down. It was a small black dog, trotting along at my feet.

'Hello! Where did you come from?' I bent down and gave him a pat. He had a square head with a white patch over one eye, and a stocky little body. He looked like a barrel on legs. 'You're only a pup! And you haven't got a collar on. Are you lost, little fella?'

The puppy cocked his head and looked at me with alert brown eyes. His tongue was hanging out, giving him a cheeky grin.

'Hugo! Don't you dare!' Jasper came marching back towards me. She had on her 'bossy big sister' face. 'You know what Mum and Dad said last time. No more stray dogs.'

I sighed. There was nothing I wanted more than my very own dog. I didn't mind what sort. Big or small, fluffy or sleek, brown or black or spotted — I didn't care. As long as it had four legs and a tail and a cheeky grin. Just like this one.

'What if he hasn't got a family to go home to? We can't just leave him here on his own . . .'

Jasper grabbed my shirt and started pulling me up the street. 'Come on. Don't encourage him.'

I gave the little dog one last pat. 'Off you go,' I said half-heartedly. 'Go home. Good boy.'

The dog sat on the road and watched, puzzled, as I walked away. Then he started trotting after me.

Frankie focussed her camera on him and took some pictures. 'He's cute,' she said, switching to another camera with a bigger lens on it. 'He's not at all camera-shy.'

The black dog jumped up and licked my hand, then raced off and picked up a stick with his mouth. He sauntered back grinning and dropped the stick at my feet.

'Hugo!' Jasper stood with her hands on her hips, glaring at me.

'What? I haven't done anything,' I said innocently. 'I can't help it if he's following me.' I bent down and threw the stick. 'Go on doggie. Off you go.'

Jasper shrugged her shoulders. 'Well, don't blame me when you get in trouble. I tried to tell you . . .'

The dog came charging back with the stick, his grin bigger than ever. His tail was wagging so hard it looked like he was about to lift off. I bent down and gave him another pat. He nuzzled my hand with his wet black nose.

'You're a smart dog, aren't you?' I murmured. 'And you've got a good nose, too. I bet you could sniff out a big story from a hundred miles away. A real scoop. In fact, maybe that's what I'll call you . . . just for now. Scoop!'

The little black dog cocked his head to one side as if he was thinking. Then he jumped up and licked my face. He liked his name!

'Good boy, Scoop,' I whispered. I stood up and tossed the stick as far as I could. He galloped off after it looking more like a piglet than a dog. 'Good boy!'

'NO — MORE — STRAYS!' thundered Dad.

'But, Dad . . .' My voice trailed off. I'd come up with every argument I could think of, but none of them worked. Even the one about needing a guard dog to protect me now that I was a reporter doing dangerous assignments.

'If the assignment is so dangerous that you need a dog, then you shouldn't be doing it,' Dad said sternly. 'No dangerous assignments, no dogs. And that's final.'

'What sort of a dog is it anyway?' asked Mum, sounding amused. 'It looks like a little black pig!'

'I think it's a Staffordshire bull terrier,' said Dad, picking Scoop up and looking closely at him.

'A male, about six months old is my guess. Looks like a pedigree. He'd be worth a bit of money, I'd say. Someone's probably out looking for him right now.'

I gave it one last try. 'Can't we just keep him until we find the real owner?'

'We could put a "Lost and Found" notice in *Street Wise*,' suggested Jasper. She added under her breath, '. . . in really small writing on the back page where nobody will see it, of course.'

I smiled gratefully at her. At least Jasper was on my side.

'I've said no, and I mean it,' repeated Dad irritably. 'Dogs are too much trouble. They cost a fortune at the vet's, and they eat food like it's going out of style.' He glared at Scoop. 'AND they do their business where someone is guaranteed to step in it.'

Jasper and I stifled a giggle. Poor Dad — his best shoes.

'Anyway, what about your goldfish?' Mum reminded us. 'They're lovely pets.'

I eyed the fish bowl with contempt. Ready, Setty and Go stared back blankly, silently mouthing BLUB-BLUB-BLUB. I knew what they were saying. They were saying: 'Dull. Dull. Dull.' That was the only word in goldfish language. It summed up their entire lives.

Jasper snorted. 'They're not pets. They're a waste of space.'

'They're boring,' I added morosely. 'They don't *do* anything.'

Scoop struggled out of Dad's arms and ran over to me. I patted him sadly. 'I guess this is goodbye, little fella. It's been nice knowing you.'

Scoop panted eagerly, his bright eyes begging me to go outside and throw a stick for him. Poor Scoop. He didn't realise that in ten seconds flat, he was going to be in the back of Dad's car going to the pound.

'While I slip out with the dog, you can tell them the good news,' I heard Dad say quietly to Mum. 'It's easier if they don't come with me to the pound. Hugo's already too attached to the dog as it is.'

I sat at the kitchen table, my eyes filling with tears as Dad picked up Scoop and walked out the back door. Jasper was right. It was just like every other time I brought a dog home. Mum and Dad never let me keep them. But Scoop was different. He was special. This time . . . this time I thought they would let him stay.

'Hugo.' It was Mum. She sat down at the table with me and gave me a hug. 'I know how much the little dog meant to you, but we just couldn't keep him.'

'His name is Scoop,' I said numbly.

Mum sighed. 'We couldn't keep Scoop, Hugo, but I've got a wonderful surprise to make up for it.'

Jasper let out a whoop. 'A surprise! Great! Can I have it too?'

I stared at my hands. The only surprise that would make me feel better was Scoop, running in the back door with a stick in his mouth.

Mum nodded. 'It's a special surprise for both of you. Dad and I are going to Singapore for a week so I can go to a law conference, and he can have a holiday from the business.'

'Singapore! Cool!' Jasper clapped her hands. 'We can eat Chinese takeaway every night and ride around in one of those rickshaw thingummies! I can pretend I'm the Queen of Sheba.' She prodded me and added grandly, 'You can be my slave-boy, Hugo.'

'Well . . . no, actually, that's not the plan,' said Mum. 'You see, Dad and I are going to Singapore on our own. It's like a second honeymoon. You and Hugo are staying behind.'

'Staying behind?' wailed Jasper. 'But that's not fair! I want to go on a rickshaw . . .'

'I couldn't care less,' I said grumpily. 'I'd rather have Scoop than a trip to Singapore any old day.'

Mum looked frazzled. 'Oh, dear. Perhaps I didn't

say this quite the right way. The reason you're not coming to Singapore is that you're going somewhere much better.' She smiled at us brightly. 'You're going to Auntie Marge's Fun Camp for Kids!'

Jasper and I were stunned.

'We don't have an Auntie Marge,' I said suspiciously.

'Well, no, of course you don't,' Mum said. 'Auntie Marge is just what the lady calls herself. She's very friendly and jolly — just like a real aunt! I've spoken to her on the phone. It's all arranged.'

Jasper looked crestfallen.

'I'd rather go in a rickshaw,' she said forlornly. 'With you and Dad. What if we don't like Auntie Marge?'

'Of course you'll like Auntie Marge,' Mum said firmly. 'You'll *love* Auntie Marge.' She stood up and started filling the kettle with water. It was her way of saying the matter was settled.

'In fact,' she said cheerily, sticking the kettle on the stove, 'I guarantee you'll have so much fun, you won't want to leave the place!'

Chapter Two

'Take the next turn left, and that should bring us back onto the highway.'

Jasper and I sat in the back of the car expectantly. Whenever Dad navigated, interesting things seemed to happen. Sometimes we ended up where we were supposed to, but usually not. Usually we had some sort of adventure — 'a major drama' as Mum called it — and then turned around and went back home. Both of us hoped that would happen this time.

'I think we're lost,' said Mum, hanging onto the steering wheel for dear life. The dirt road was so bumpy we were bouncing around all over the place.

'What do you mean?' demanded Dad, looking up from the map. He was starting to sound stressed. 'According to the map, this should lead us back to the highway. What's that up ahead?'

'It's a paddock,' replied Mum, through gritted teeth. 'With cows in it. You've taken us onto private property.'

'I hate to break it to you, Dad, but we're lost,' said Jasper cheerfully.

'They'll have to send the rescue helicopter to find us!' I yelped excitedly. 'I hope we've got enough food to see us through!'

'Don't be ridiculous,' said Dad crossly. 'We're not lost, we're just . . . taking the scenic route. We'll be back on the highway in no time.'

I checked my watch, and nudged Jasper jubilantly. Nearly ten o'clock. If we didn't find Auntie Marge's Fun Camp soon, Mum and Dad would miss their plane to Singapore, and we could all go home again. Toby and Frankie would be pleased. They thought they'd be putting together the newspaper on their own this week.

Mum stopped the car and looked over Dad's shoulder. She sighed patiently and turned the map the right way round.

'It helps if the map isn't upside down, darling heart.' She gave him a kiss on the cheek and started the engine once more. 'Now. Let's try again.'

'Excuse me, can you please tell us where Auntie Marge's Fun Camp is?' Mum asked.

The old man stopped his bicycle and peered in the car window. 'A fun camp? No ma'am, I can't say I've heard of a fun camp hereabouts,' he said, shaking his head.

Jasper and I grinned at each other. Things were looking hopeful. If we couldn't find the fun camp, Mum and Dad would have to take us to Singapore with them. Or even better, they might take us home again. Then we could get back to finding stories for *Street Wise*. Neither of us wanted to waste a whole week at some silly fun camp — we had a newspaper to put out!

Dad leaned over and waved the map at him. 'But this is Willowvale, isn't it?' he asked desperately. 'That's the address we've got for Auntie Marge's Fun Camp. Ninety-five Yabbie Creek Road, Willowvale.'

The old man took his cap off and scratched his head. 'Well, now, this here is Willowvale, all right,' he said slowly. 'But there ain't no fun camp at that address. That's Pegleg Paddy's place. He keeps dogs. Him and his mother, Old Marge.'

My ears pricked up. Dogs?

'Prize-winning dogs,' added the old man, seeing

my interest. 'At least they used to win prizes — until all the trouble.'

What did he mean, trouble? This was starting to sound interesting.

Mum turned to Dad, looking worried. 'Maybe there's been some mistake, Nick.'

Dad pulled out a glossy brochure. 'That's impossible. Look — it's all here. Even pictures. And we both spoke to Mrs Steggles on the telephone. Maybe it's a brand new business, that's why nobody's heard of it.'

The old man let out a loud cackle. 'Fun camp, my foot. The Puppy Factory — that's what we call it around here. Pegleg Paddy's Puppy Factory.' He pushed his whiskery old face close to mine. 'The barkin' drives some people bonkers, y'know.'

I pulled away, wrinkling my nose. The old man didn't smell too fresh. Maybe he was a bit bonkers himself.

'Yes, well, thank you for your help,' said Mum hurriedly. 'We have a plane to catch, so we'll say good day to you.'

The tyres screeched as we roared off down the road.

'They'll have to come with us to Singapore.' Mum's voice sounded panicky. 'There's no other choice. I'm not leaving them at some dog kennel.'

'Now, now, Jennifer, just calm down,' said Dad. 'Don't let that horrible old bloke upset you. There's probably a very good explanation. Let's just go and see.'

I stared out of the window as Mum stepped on the brake and brought the car to a halt. We were there.

In front of us was a giant iron gate. Across the top was a sign saying 'Auntie Marge's Fun Camp for Kids'. It was perfectly painted in big, blue lettering — except somebody had added a couple of letters to the front of 'fun'. If you looked closely, you could see it now said 'un-Fun Camp'. The extra letters were untidy, and black, with dribbles of paint running down from them. Maybe it was a joke. Mum and Dad hadn't noticed, and before I could point it out to them, the gates suddenly slid open.

'Look, no hands,' joked Dad. 'I didn't even press a button. Must be electric gates controlled from the house.'

'Well, it's very secure, that's one good thing,' said Mum, sounding a little happier. 'At least we know the children are safe.'

As we drove through, I saw a video camera mounted on the top of the gate-post, its red eye blinking at us.

The road wound around a small hill and then straight up through a long avenue of pine trees.

'It's a bit gloomy, isn't it?' said Dad. 'If it was my place I'd get rid of those pines and plant some nice gum trees.'

I hunched further back into the car seat. The place was starting to give me the creeps. Jasper was quiet too. I could tell she didn't like it either.

'Oh, look at the house!' cried Mum.

I looked up. The pine trees had ended, and looming in front of us was a house that was straight out of a monster movie.

It was a big, grey stone place that looked at least a hundred years old. There were turrets and towers sticking out all over the place, covered in thick green ivy. I craned my neck out of the car window and counted the storeys. One, two . . . three, if you counted the attic with its tall pointy roof. Three storeys high! Even the richest family in Blue Rock, the Fitzherberts, only had two storeys. It was the sort of place that King Arthur, a few wicked witches and Frankenstein's monster could live in quite happily without ever having to see each other.

'Isn't it gorgeous?' sighed Mum, getting out of the car. 'A real Gothic mansion.'

'A real House of Horrors, more like it,' I said under my breath.

'It needs a lot of work done to it,' said Dad, eyeing it critically. Jasper and I scrambled out of the car after him. 'But it's certainly got potential. Whack a new roof and a coat of paint on it, and it'd look a million dollars.'

The four of us stood there, taking it all in. In the distance, I could hear the sound of dogs barking. Lots of them. Hundreds, even. So the old man was telling the truth. They kept dogs here as well. The Puppy Factory, he'd called it.

'Look up there,' Jasper shouted, pointing towards one of the turrets. Two stone heads — carved into grimacing, twisted faces — leered back at us.

'Gargoyles,' Dad said. 'Ugly, aren't they? They're supposed to keep evil spirits away.'

Jasper shuddered. 'They're enough to scare anyone away. Not that they'd need them. Listen to those dogs!'

Staring at the gargoyles, I saw something move out of the corner of my eye. I spun towards the attic window and saw a girl with long snow white hair standing at the window. For a split second our eyes locked. But when I blinked, she was gone.

'That girl! In the attic! Did you see her?' I shook Jasper impatiently.

'What girl? I was looking at the gargoyles.' She

squinted up at the attic. 'There's nobody there now. It was probably a shadow or something.'

'It wasn't, I'm sure of it. There was a girl there, she looked sad and lonely . . .' My voice trailed off lamely. Maybe she was right. There certainly wasn't anybody standing at the attic window now. Or maybe . . . maybe the old place was haunted.

'Let's get out of here.' I grabbed Mum and Dad and tried to pull them back towards the car. 'Come on, I'm scared . . .'

Just then, there was a terrible creaking noise from the House of Horrors. The big, wooden front door was opening slowly. I stood, glued to the spot, half-expecting to see a Frankenstein monster lurching out of it, with a hump and a bad leg.

But it wasn't a monster. It was a round, elderly lady with her grey hair in a bun. She was wearing enormous spectacles with pink frames, and a pink and white gingham frock. Her hands looked like they were covered in flour, and she was wiping them on her white lacy apron as she walked towards us.

'Hello there! You must be the Lilley family! Nice to meet you!'

Mum and Dad looked at each other, relieved.

'And you must be Mrs Steggles. We were just admiring your house,' said Dad politely.

'Please, call me Auntie Marge — everybody

does.' The old lady smiled sweetly at us. She looked like she should have been living in the Gingerbread Cottage, not the House of Horrors. 'Hello, Hugo . . . Hello, Jasper. Your father's told me all about you.' Auntie Marge held out her hand for us to shake. 'Please excuse the flour. I've been baking Anzac biscuits for the children all morning!'

Mum laughed. 'I don't know what we were worried about,' she said to Dad. She turned to Auntie Marge, 'You obviously run a very fine establishment here.'

Within five minutes, Mum and Dad and Auntie Marge were chatting away like they'd known each other all their lives. Even Jasper was joining in. But I couldn't say a word. Something was bothering me. It was Auntie Marge's fingernails. When she gave us her hand to shake, I noticed that they were black with dirt, and badly bitten. It just didn't fit with Auntie Marge's squeaky-clean image. And why would her nails be black if she'd had her hands in flour? It didn't make sense.

'My, you're a quiet boy, aren't you?' trilled Auntie Marge, chucking me under the chin.

'He's a little shy until you get to know him,' said Mum. 'But it doesn't take long. And I understand you keep dogs? Hugo's very fond of them.'

'Well, he'll be happy here, then,' replied Auntie

Marge. 'Because I have lots and lots of dogs! And I always need a hand to look after them. Now, leave the bags at the front door, and come and see my excellent playground facilities.'

She led us around the back of the house.

'Cheer up, Hugo,' whispered Jasper fiercely. 'The old duck's not too bad. And it's only for a week.'

Auntie Marge pointed proudly at a large wire enclosure in the distance. From where we stood I could see that inside, there were swings and monkey-bars and slides and roundabouts, with kids crawling all over them. I could see other kids, standing at the wire fence, shouting and waving at us. It looked liked a pretty good playground. I started to feel a bit more cheerful. Maybe it wouldn't be torture after all ... even if Auntie Marge did have dirty fingernails.

'It's not all fun and games, of course.' Auntie Marge dimpled sweetly. 'I believe in teaching children to help around the house. They all have simple chores to perform before they play.'

'Excellent!' Dad looked pleased. 'Maybe you can teach them to keep their rooms tidy. That would be a real bonus!'

'Er ... just one question, Auntie Marge,' asked Mum hesitantly. 'Why is the playground caged in? I mean, you're in the middle of the countryside here ...'

'Security, my dear.' Auntie Marge pursed her lips. 'There are lots of dams and creeks around here, and I'd hate any of the little darlings to escape . . . I mean, to fall in and drown.'

'Oh, of course.' Mum nodded. 'Very sensible.'

'We have electrified fences around the entire property as well,' continued Auntie Marge. 'Not so much to keep the children *in*, but to keep undesirable characters *out*. I'm sure you understand.'

'Absolutely. We're very impressed,' said Dad. 'You obviously run a very tight ship here. Now, my wife and I have a plane to catch, so perhaps we should pay you some money and be on our way.'

'Money? Oh, of course, I almost forgot,' said Auntie Marge, laughing heartily. 'I do this for love, you see — I really hate taking money for it. But since you've reminded me . . .'

She watched closely as Dad brought out his chequebook.

'I only take cash,' said Auntie Marge. Her tone of voice was suddenly very different. It was almost . . . rude. Then she smiled and switched back to her gentle, refined voice. 'Cash only, dear Mr Lilley. We did discuss it on the phone.'

'Of course we did. My mistake,' apologised Dad. 'Here you are, Auntie Marge. Thank you so much for taking these two rascals off our hands. We'll see you in a week's time. Be good, kids!'

Auntie Marge stuffed the wad of notes in her pocket and waved as Mum and Dad drove off down through the pine forest and then out through the front gates.

I watched them go with a terrible sinking feeling in my stomach. I thought of the spy camera on the front gate. Auntie Marge's dirty fingernails. The caged-in playground. My reporter's gut instinct told me that Auntie Marge's Fun Camp wasn't as fun as it seemed. But it was too late now to do anything about it — Mum and Dad were gone.

In the distance we heard the electric gate slide shut.

Auntie Marge stopped waving and turned to us. She wasn't smiling any more. In fact she looked mean and nasty.

'You two — get in the house!' she barked. 'My floors need scrubbing!'

Chapter Three

'MOVE IT!' yelled Auntie Marge, sounding just like a sergeant major.

Jasper flicked her plaits crossly. 'That's not a very nice way to talk to us,' she said haughtily. 'You should say please if you . . .'

Jasper didn't even get to finish her sentence. Auntie Marge grabbed the two of us by our sleeves and dragged us up the stairs. For an old lady she was as strong as an ox.

'Into the kitchen, you little grubs!' she roared. 'I want that floor so clean I can eat off it.'

'But we want to go to the playground . . .' Jasper started to protest.

I shook my head at her as Auntie Marge pulled us up a long dark hallway. 'Don't answer back,' I whispered. My hunch had been right. Auntie Marge wasn't the sweet old lady she pretended to be.

'There!' Auntie Marge pushed us through a doorway. 'Mops, buckets and scrubbing brushes in the corner. I'll be back in one hour to check your work — and it better be good. If it's not . . . no dinner!'

'But we're supposed to be having fun,' wailed Jasper, before I could stop her. 'We're not supposed to be working. I want to go home . . .'

Auntie Marge's eyes narrowed into spiteful slits.

'If I hear one more word out of you, girlie,' she said slowly, 'I'll put you on toilet duty for the rest of the week.'

Jasper shut her mouth quickly.

Auntie Marge glared at the two of us. 'Well, what are you waiting for? GET TO WORK!'

She strode off, slamming the door shut behind her. We waited until the sound of Auntie Marge's heavy footsteps faded away.

'Gosh,' I gulped. 'So this is what she meant by simple chores. I bet Mum and Dad didn't know it was going to be like this.'

Jasper's face was flushed with anger and confusion.

'I don't understand!' she fumed. 'Auntie Marge

seemed so nice when we got here. Now she's being horrible. Wait until we tell Mum and Dad.'

I looked at my watch.

'Well, we won't be telling them for a long time.' I shook my head glumly. 'Their plane takes off for Singapore in ten minutes. I guess we just have to make the best of it. They won't be back to pick us up for a week.'

A whole week. My heart sank just thinking about it. Well, at least Jasper and I had each other. If only Toby and Frankie were here too, it would almost be an adventure.

I looked around. We were in an enormous kitchen, with cupboards right up to the ceiling and a giant fireplace at one end. In the middle there was a long wooden table with wooden benches on either side. An open packet of flour lay on its side, its insides spilling out onto the table.

'Look at this stove. It must be a hundred years old.' Jasper tapped it. 'Solid iron.' She opened a trap door at the front of it. 'Oh, look. It runs on firewood. I wonder who chops it all up?'

We looked at each other and groaned. Probably us.

Jasper started opening the cupboards and peering inside.

'Any biscuits?' I asked hopefully. It felt like a decade since breakfast.

'No. But look at this.' Jasper sounded puzzled. She flung open a cupboard door. 'Dog food. Hundreds and hundreds of tins of dog food.'

A terrible thought struck me.

'You don't think we have to eat dog food, do you?'

Jasper shook her head. 'Even Auntie Marge couldn't be that mean. It must be for her dogs.'

Of course! I'd forgotten about the dogs. They'd been barking in the background for so long I'd stopped hearing them.

'I wonder where she keeps them?' I grabbed the end of one of the wooden benches and dragged it over to the window so I could look out. 'Here. Help me up.'

I stood on tippy-toes and peered over the edge of the windowsill. Everything in this house was so big. It was like living in the Land of the Giants.

'Well, hurry up,' demanded Jasper impatiently. 'What can you see?'

I gazed out of the window. The first thing I saw was the caged playground. It was empty; the gate chained and padlocked shut. Where had all the kids gone? We'd seen them playing in it before. They couldn't have just disappeared ... could they? I thought of the spooky old house we were in, and shivered. There was something mysterious going on here, and I had no idea what it was.

My eye moved on to a long whitewashed building about twenty metres away from the playground. That seemed to be where the barking was coming from. There was no sign of any dogs. They must be inside it.

'I think I've found the kennels,' I told Jasper. 'They're inside a big white building almost as big as our house in Blue Rock.' A sudden wave of homesickness swept through me. It was only a few hours since we left home that morning but already it seemed like a lifetime.

Suddenly, my thoughts snapped back to the present. The door to the long white building was opening. Someone was coming out. I strained my eyes. It wasn't Auntie Marge; it was a man, carrying a sack.

'Quick, come up here and have a look.' Jasper jumped up on the bench beside me. We watched as the man carried the sack towards a rusty red jeep parked next to the playground. He was short and stocky, with a bald head and a bushy beard. He was wearing black wrap-around sunglasses and a faded blue singlet that showed off his hairy arms.

'I wonder who that is?' asked Jasper. 'He looks like a bikie bandit. And why is he walking like that?'

I took a closer look. The man had a strange way of walking. It wasn't exactly a limp — more like a stiff leg. But it was the sack that caught my eye. Whatever was in it was moving.

'He's got something alive in that sack,' I said. 'Look, it's wriggling all over the place.'

The bearded man lifted the sack carefully into the back of the jeep. As he did, something small and brown squirmed out of the top of it and jumped to the ground.

'It's a puppy!' I cried. 'He's got a sack full of puppies, and one of them's escaped!'

The bearded man picked up the pup by the scruff of its neck and lowered it gently into the sack again. Then he got into the jeep and drove off.

Jasper and I looked at each other, perplexed. Things were getting more and more bizarre by the second. But before we had time to speak, someone beat us to it.

'Hey! What are youse doing up there?'

We spun around. Standing there with his legs apart and his hands on his hips was a skinny boy with sandy hair and the biggest, orangest freckles I'd ever seen in my life. He grinned at us and stuck out a grubby hand.

'G'day. My name's Tyson. Who are youse?'

'The first thing youse need to know about this place,' Tyson began, 'is that there are two sets of rules: one for them, and one for us. The trick is knowing how to work the system.'

Our new friend was sitting cross-legged on top of the long wooden table, giving us the lowdown. I was busy taking notes. Luckily, I never went anywhere without my reporter's notebook. You never knew when it was going to come in handy — and if Jasper and I were going to survive a week at Auntie Marge's, we needed all the information we could get.

'Who are "they"?' asked Jasper. 'I thought it was only Auntie Marge.'

'Negative.' Tyson shook his head. 'The old boiler has a son, Paddy. Pegleg Paddy they call him. He's got a wooden leg. He lost his real leg in a motorbike accident. He's rough as guts and as mean as a feral pig. Spends all his time with the dogs, or mucking about on the computer.'

Of course. Pegleg Paddy's Puppy Factory — that's what the old man on the bicycle had called it. That must have been him we'd seen earlier with the sack of puppies. The wooden leg would explain his unusual walk.

'The thing to remember with Pegleg is that he can't move very fast,' Tyson continued. He seemed to know everything. 'So if you ever bump into him — run for your life. If he catches you, you're dead meat.'

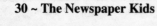

Seeing our alarm, he waved his hand reassuringly. 'It's okay, I've been here two whole weeks and he's never caught anyone yet.'

Phew. That was a relief. But there was one thing that was really puzzling me.

'Why do they call this a Fun Camp?' I asked. 'By the sounds of it, it's no fun at all. And why run a camp for kids if you hate kids?'

Tyson chuckled. 'Money, Hugo. The only reason old Marge and Paddy run it is to make money, so they can afford to keep their dogs. Plus they use us kids as slaves. They'd never be able to keep the dogs and the house in order if it wasn't for us.'

Jasper and I exchanged worried looks. So that was the reason the playground was locked up like a cage. According to Tyson, the only time the kids were allowed to use it was when someone was being dropped off or picked up by parents. Old Marge and Paddy just wanted to make a good impression on the mums and dads. As soon as they left, the kids were herded out and put back to work — cleaning and patching up the old house, chopping firewood, mowing the grass, and waiting on Auntie Marge hand and foot. Every day, half the kids were rostered on to exercise and feed the dogs, and clean out the kennels. And there was no point trying to escape. The entire property was surrounded by an electric fence.

'We did yell out and try to warn you when we saw you arrive this morning,' Tyson continued. 'But you didn't hear. And even if you did, you wouldn't have believed us.' He pointed to the spilled flour on the table. 'Auntie Marge always puts on such a good act — right down to rubbing her hands in flour so the parents think she's been baking.'

That explained her dirty fingernails. I chewed on my pen thoughtfully. This was starting to sound like a good story. If only Toby and Frankie were here . . .

'But don't the parents get angry when they find out?' asked Jasper curiously.

Tyson shrugged. 'I don't think they believe what the kids tell them. Auntie Marge tells the parents the kids have to do a few chores — I guess they think their little darlings are just exaggerating. Besides, as long as we don't starve to death, Auntie Marge isn't really breaking any law.'

That reminded me. My stomach rumbled ominously.

'Speaking of starving,' I ventured, 'I don't suppose you know if there are any biscuits around here?'

'Ah. Food.' Tyson jumped off the table and beckoned us over to the cupboards. He opened

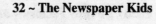

one of the bottom ones with a flourish. I looked inside eagerly.

'Oh. Brussels sprouts. And tins of baked beans.' My empty stomach ached with disappointment. 'Is that it?'

'That's what they give us every night for dinner,' Tyson informed us. 'Burnt porridge for breakfast — or sometimes raw porridge, depending which kid's on kitchen detail — and baked beans and Brussels sprouts for dinner.'

Jasper wrinkled her nose. 'Gross.'

I stared at the cupboard with a heavy heart. It was enough to keep us alive and healthy . . . but Brussels sprouts? The vegetable I hated more than anything else on the planet. There was no doubt about it — Auntie Marge was a very cruel woman.

'She's mean,' agreed Tyson cheerfully, reading my mind. 'But like I said — you have to know how to work the system.'

He grinned, and pointed up to a cupboard that was way, way out of our reach. 'That's Auntie Marge's special pantry up there. It's full of goodies. More food than you could eat in a lifetime. She uses a ladder to get to it.'

I cast my eye desperately around the kitchen. 'So where is it? Where's the ladder?'

'It's locked away, but we can get just as high by dragging the table over, putting the bench on it, then a chair on top of the bench.'

'Sounds like we're building the Leaning Tower of Pisa,' said Jasper doubtfully.

'The Leaning Tower of Pieces of Furniture,' I corrected her. My eyes lit up. 'Well, what are we waiting for?'

Two minutes later we were munching on chocolate bars, with a jar of Anzac biscuits on stand-by. But just as I was reaching in to grab another one, I heard a noise that struck terror into my heart.

Thump. Thump. Thump. Heavy footsteps, walking down the hallway.

'It's the old boiler!' yelped Tyson. 'I'm outta here!' He stuffed a handful of biscuits down his T-shirt and slipped out the back door like a shadow.

Thump. Thump. Thump. The footsteps were getting closer.

'That floor better be clean!' I heard Auntie Marge yell. 'Clean as a whistle or it's toilet duty for both of you!'

Jasper and I froze with terror. The evidence was everywhere. Jasper had crumbs all around her mouth. I looked at my hands — they were smeared with chocolate. Not to mention the

Leaning Tower. Any second now Auntie Marge was going to walk in the door, and there was nothing we could do about it.

'I'm coming!' thundered Auntie Marge. The kitchen door rattled on its hinges.

You didn't have to be a rocket scientist to know that we were in big, big trouble.

Chapter Four

'**Q**uick! There's no time to lose!'

Jasper flew across the room and grabbed a chair from beside the fireplace. She dragged it across the floor and tilted it until the back of the chair was jammed under the door handle.

'Don't just stand there, Hugo,' whispered Jasper furiously. 'Put the food away and get all the furniture back in place. This won't hold forever.'

I hardly heard her. Something — a movement at the window — had caught my eye. It looked like a flash of snow white hair. But when I spun around to face it squarely, there was nothing there.

Auntie Marge rattled the door handle.

'What's going on here?'

The sound of her voice cut through my thoughts, and I sprang into action. Time enough later to find out who the face at the window was.

'Where did you learn to do that thing with the chair?' I asked Jasper admiringly as I closed the cupboard on Auntie Marge's special pantry and climbed down from the table.

'The movies,' answered Jasper abruptly. 'Here, I'll grab this end of the table, you push from the other end.'

Our hearts racing, we moved the table back into the centre of the kitchen and lifted the bench off it.

'Open up, you brats!' yelled Auntie Marge, banging on the door. 'I know you're in there!'

'The door's stuck, Auntie,' Jasper sang out sweetly. She ran over and rattled the handle. 'I'm trying my hardest but I just can't open it.'

She turned to me urgently. 'The crumbs! Wipe them up, hurry! If she sees them she'll know what we've been up to.'

I swept the crumbs into my hand and rinsed them down the sink, checking to make sure all the evidence was gone. Auntie Marge had started throwing herself against the door; it wouldn't be long before the chair gave way.

'What about the floor?' I'd completely forgotten

we were meant to clean it until then. Auntie Marge would be furious.

Jasper shook her head desperately. 'There's no time.'

BANG! The door bulged inwards as Auntie Marge charged at it like a footie player.

'Once more ought to do it,' I heard her say. I closed my eyes and said a quick prayer. At least she wouldn't know we'd been into her special pantry. That would have spoiled it for all the kids.

Just then I heard the front doorbell ring.

'Now, who could that be?' muttered Auntie Marge from the other side of the door. Her heavy footsteps thumped off down the long hallway.

'Saved by the bell!' I looked at Jasper jubilantly. 'Quick, take the chair away so she doesn't know we jammed the door on purpose. I'll throw a bit of water on the floor and move the mop around. Hopefully, she won't look too closely.'

We didn't have long. Within thirty seconds Auntie Marge's footsteps were tramping back up the hallway.

'Darned kids, playing tricks again,' she grumbled.

I peeked through the keyhole. Auntie Marge was on the other side. She was breathing heavily, and snorting like a bull. As I watched, she took two deep breaths and started running towards the door.

'Look out, here she comes!' Jasper and I stepped out of the way.

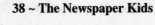

'CHA-A-A-RGE!' bellowed Auntie Marge. The next minute the door burst open and she came flying through like a missile. Jasper and I watched as Auntie Marge hurtled through the air and landed with a giant crash on the floor.

'Are you all right?' I asked politely, trying not to laugh.

'Does it look like I'm all right, you stupid boy?' snapped Auntie Marge. 'Here — help me up.' She struggled to her feet, rubbing her head, and glared at us. 'It's all your fault. What did you do to the door?'

'Nothing, Auntie,' said Jasper innocently. 'It just got jammed, honestly.'

Auntie Marge looked at us suspiciously. 'Hmmm. I'll have to get Paddy to look at it. Now, what about this floor?'

Jasper and I held our breath. So far, so good. Auntie Marge had believed our story about the door . . . with any luck, she'd be fooled by the few damp streaks I'd managed to paint with my wet mop.

Auntie Marge walked slowly around the room, breathing loudly through her nostrils. Every few paces, she paused, and peered at the floor through her big spectacles.

Finally, she stopped in front of us.

'This — floor— is — filthy.'

Auntie Marge spat out the words. She drew herself up to her full height — which wasn't that much taller than Jasper, but she still looked pretty scary.

'You are very lazy children!' thundered Auntie Marge, 'Ungrateful! Slothful!'

Jasper and I quailed. This whole experience was getting worse by the minute, and there didn't seem to be anything we could do about it. Until Mum and Dad got back from Singapore, we were stuck.

Auntie Marge strode to the back door and threw it open. A blast of cold air rushed in. I shivered. This old house was as draughty as a graveyard.

'Petronella!' yelled Auntie Marge. 'Petronella Duff! Get in here!'

Within five seconds I heard the sound of running footsteps, then a solid, square-shaped girl with black hair appeared in the doorway.

She saw Auntie Marge and snapped to attention.

'Camp Monitor Duff, reporting for duty!'

I glanced at Jasper and rolled my eyes. Camp Monitor must mean she was somehow in charge, like the class prefects at school. I took a closer look at her. Her dark hair was pretty, but her mouth was turned down and surly. She looked a bit older than us — maybe twelve. Another one of the camp's inmates, I guessed. How many others were there?

'Take these two upstairs to the attic,' ordered Auntie Marge. 'A bit of solitary confinement and a few hunger pangs might improve their attitude to work. Then get back here and make me a cup of tea. I'm ready to die of thirst.'

'Yes, Auntie Marge,' Petronella replied obediently. She looked at us and scowled. 'You heard her! Get moving!'

Solitary confinement? The attic? My heart sank. I remembered the face I'd seen at the attic window. The blonde girl with the sad look in her eyes. Was she the same one who had looked in the window at us just then? Who was she, and why did she look so sad? Maybe she'd been sent to solitary confinement, just like us, and they'd forgotten about her . . . and now she came back as a ghost . . .

Jasper nudged me. 'Come on, Hugo.'

I shook myself out of my daydream, and followed Petronella up the stairs.

'That's the boys' dormitory.' Petronella jerked her head towards a room off the first landing. I peeked inside. It was plain but clean, with two rows of narrow beds neatly made up. Petronella gave me a push. 'Stop dawdling. You won't be sleeping there tonight.'

'What do you mean?' I'd decided I didn't like Petronella one bit. She was very unfriendly.

'Because you'll be sleeping in the attic, that's why.' Petronella turned to us with a smirk. 'It's haunted, you know.'

A cold hand of fear closed around my stomach. So I'd been right.

'Oh, rubbish,' scoffed Jasper, flicking her plaits. 'There's no such thing as ghosts. Everyone knows that.'

'Yeah! Ghosts are just made-up things to scare people,' I added, trying to convince myself as well as Petronella. 'They're like monsters in a dream. All you have to do is walk up to them and say "I don't believe in you", and they go away.'

Petronella sneered at me. 'Fine. Then we won't send anyone to rescue you when we hear you screaming tonight. And don't expect any dinner. We don't do room service here.'

Jasper gave my elbow a squeeze. I could tell she disliked Petronella as much as I did.

The stairs were old and ricketty, and they seemed to go on forever. Finally, at the top of the third flight, we stopped outside a door. Petronella took a large key out of her pocket.

'How come you get to be Camp Monitor?' I asked curiously, watching her open the door.

Petronella puffed out her chest. 'Because this is my fourth time at the camp. Auntie Marge trusts me.

I tell her everything that goes on — so don't let me catch you doing anything you shouldn't!'

'A snitch,' muttered Jasper under her breath.

I looked around the room. So this was the attic. It was a small, bare room with sloping ceilings and a single window. That must have been where I saw the sad-faced girl standing when we first arrived. In the corner I saw a pile of blankets. That was it. Apart from the blankets, the room was empty.

Something was niggling me about Petronella. 'Why do you stay here so much?' I asked. Frankly, I was amazed anyone would come back to this horrible place a second time, let alone a third and a fourth.

For some reason Petronella exploded. She turned on me, her eyes blazing. 'Because my parents are very important people,' she yelled. 'And they're very, very busy doing important things. So there!'

She stormed out of the attic and slammed the door loudly behind her. Before I had time to say 'Well, excuse me for *living*', we heard the key turn in the lock.

'We have to escape.'

I was still staring out of the window when Jasper spoke. From three storeys up, I had a good view. I could see the long driveway we had come up with Mum and Dad, then further out, the electric fence that encircled the whole property, and the big front gate. In the background, I could hear the dogs barking.

'I don't see how,' I said glumly. 'Even if we managed to get past the security camera and out of the front gate, how would we find our way home?'

Jasper was pacing around the small room, chewing thoughtfully on her plaits.

'We need to contact Toby. He'll know what to do.'

Of course! I'd almost forgotten we were only half of a team. The other half — Toby and Frankie — were safe at home in Blue Rock. Right now, they were probably hard at work on the next edition of *Street Wise*, thinking we were having a brilliant time at the Fun Camp.

Ha! I thought wryly. If only they knew the truth. This wasn't a Fun Camp. It was a Hell Camp!

Suddenly, a thought struck me. There *was* a way to let people know the truth about Auntie Marge's Fun Camp. It was so obvious I hadn't even thought about it. I'd write a story for the newspaper!

The more I thought about it, the more excited I got. Here I was, an investigative reporter with a great story sitting right under my nose. I could see the headline now: WELCOME TO HELL CAMP — an exclusive report by Hugo Lilley.

'You know, I think we're onto a good story here,' I told Jasper. 'But you're right — we have to get out

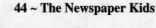

of here. If Toby and Frankie know we're in trouble, they'll think of a way to help us.'

'There's always the phone,' Jasper suggested. 'If we can get to it, we can call for help.'

'Good idea,' I nodded. Then I remembered something. Tyson had told us Pegleg Paddy spent a lot of time on the computer. 'Hey, I bet you anything their computer is on the Internet! If we can't call Toby on the phone, we'll E-mail him!'

'Excellent!' Jasper was as excited as I was. Suddenly, things didn't seem so bad. We had a plan. First, to escape. Then, to write a story to let the world know the truth about Auntie Marge's Fun Camp for Kids. It wasn't much — but it was a start.

'It's almost an adventure, if you think about it.' It was two hours later, and the sun was going down fast. I sat on the windowsill and watched as our only source of light slipped below the horizon. There was no electric light in the attic and neither of us had brought our miniature Swiss Army torches.

'Some adventure,' replied Jasper crossly. The excitement of our escape plan was starting to fade as the hours dragged on. Also, we were starting to get hungry. The thought of waiting until breakfast time for our next meal was very depressing, and I knew we had to do something to take our minds off it.

'Come on.' I jumped up. 'Let's make up our beds while we can still see. We can use some blankets as a mattress and the others as covers.'

Just as we finished, we heard a loud ruckus coming from below. The sound of a car screeching to a halt, a door slamming, a man shouting.

I rushed back to the window.

'It's Pegleg Paddy,' I told Jasper. 'He's getting that sack out of the back of his jeep.'

I struggled to get the old, stiff window open so I could hear what was going on.

'Ma! Ma, come and look!' I heard Paddy say. 'I got a good one, and I didn't even have to pinch him! Picked him up at the pound!'

I watched as Auntie Marge bustled over and looked inside the sack, and heard her squeal with delight.

'Ooh, he's a little beauty!' she cried, reaching in and pulling out a squirming bundle. 'He'll be worth a bit!'

'Another dog,' I reported back to Jasper. 'A little black puppy.'

I strained my eyes and took a closer look. From three storeys up in the fading light it was hard to see, but there was something . . . well, something *familiar* . . . about the little dog.

As I watched, he wriggled out of Marge's hands and ran barking into the darkness, emerging two seconds later with a stick in his mouth.

I nearly fell out of the window with shock.

'It's . . . it's Scoop!' I breathed.

'WHAT!' Jasper rushed over and pushed me out of the way to have a stickybeak. 'It can't be . . .'

'SCOOP! SCOOP!' I yelled out, forgetting where I was.

Auntie Marge and Paddy stopped talking and looked around. The little dog stopped in its tracks too, and stood as still as a statue with its head cocked, listening.

'What was that?' Marge said nervously.

'Just one of them darned kids, probably,' replied Paddy gruffly. 'Best I put the mutt in the bag and get him to the kennel. It's getting chilly.'

He picked up the little dog by the scruff of its neck.

'SCOOP!' I shouted desperately. *Look up, fella*, I willed him.

The little black dog seemed to prick up his ears — then suddenly looked straight up at the window. In the split second before he disappeared into Pegleg Paddy's sack, our eyes met, and I knew I was right.

It was Scoop. And he knew it was me.

But I barely had time to think about it. Jasper was pulling at my sleeve and pointing at the door. I turned to look — and thought at first I was dreaming.

There on the floor, just inside the locked door, was a tray. On it, there were two plates piled high with steaming hot food, two sets of cutlery and two napkins.

I rubbed my eyes and opened them again, half expecting the food to have disappeared. But it was still there — and it smelled fantastic. No doubt about it — it was real.

I shivered, half with fear, half with excitement. Someone — or some*thing* — was helping us out. The question was — who, or what, was it?

Chapter Five

'**I** don't get it,' I whispered to Jasper.

A ladleful of gluggy porridge whistled through the air and plopped onto my plate. I waited until the boy serving it moved on to the next person. 'That tray was gone when we woke up this morning — and the door was still locked,' I added.

Jasper sniffed her porridge and screwed up her nose. 'Search me. Whoever brought it up must have come back when we were asleep. Urrggh! This stuff looks awful.'

'You two! No talking!'

Petronella Duff rapped her spoon sharply on the table and glowered at us. There was no sign of

Auntie Marge or Pegleg Paddy in the kitchen. I guessed they were sleeping in.

I felt someone kick my leg and looked across the table. It was Tyson. He winked and pushed the jug of milk towards me. At least that was decent — fresh and hot. I drowned my revolting porridge in it until it looked like a small grey island in a steaming sea of white.

As we ate in silence I sneaked furtive looks at the other kids at the table. There were twelve of us altogether; six on one side, five on the other, and Commandant Duff at the head of the table where she could see everyone. Apart from Tyson and Petronella, I didn't know any of the others. A couple of them had fair hair, but it wasn't snow white like the girl at the attic window. Once again, I wondered if I had really seen her, or if she was just a figment of my imagination.

'Okay, pay attention everyone.' It was Petronella again, rapping the spoon on the table. 'I'm going to read out the job roster for the day. You know the drill — form two lines by the door. Kennel staff on one, everybody else on the other. ATTEN-SHUN!'

Everyone leapt to their feet and stood stiff and straight like soldiers. Jasper and I hesitated, then did the same. We'd already made a pact to blend in as much as possible, so we could plan our escape without being noticed. Hopefully, if we kept out of trouble, we'd be able to get to the phone or the computer today and contact Toby.

Petronella unfolded a piece of paper and began calling out names.

'Emily — dog washing. Nicholas — kitchen duty. Hamish, Lucy-Kate and Tyson — walking the dogs.'

As each kid's name was called out, they walked over to the door and stood obediently in line. I watched closely, trying to memorise the names so I could interview the kids later for my story. Meanwhile, I was keeping my fingers crossed that I'd be on kennel duty. That way, it would be easier for me to find Scoop.

'Annabel, Isaac and Tom — house cleaning. Robert — feeding the dogs and cleaning the kennel. Jasper — toilet duty. Hugo — weeding.'

Jasper groaned loudly as she joined the end of the line. I followed, trying not to show my disappointment. There was no doubt Jasper had scored the rough end of the pineapple, but I felt almost as bad. If I wasn't on kennel duty, how was I going to see Scoop?

Tyson nudged me as we lined up. 'How was solitary?'

'We survived,' I whispered back. A thought struck me. 'Hey — was it you who rang the doorbell and saved our necks yesterday? And did you bring us that food last night?'

Tyson checked to make sure Petronella wasn't looking, then shook his head. 'Not me. It was probably Flossie. She's the only guardian angel round here.'

'Flossie?'

'Yeah, Flossie Fleabags. She . . .'

Tyson broke off as Petronella stalked past with a bright silver whistle in her hand. Flossie Fleabags? What kind of a name was that? I made up my mind to investigate later. Right now, there was a more urgent problem. I had to get into the other line and find Scoop.

'Kennel staff, march to your work station and wait there for your orders. The rest of you, follow me,' bellowed Petronella. She gave a shrill blast on the whistle and strode out the back door.

It was now or never.

'Tyson, swap places with me! Hurry! While she's not looking!'

Tyson turned around, surprised. His line was starting to move off.

'I'll explain later,' I promised. 'Please — it's important.'

Tyson looked around quickly, then grinned. 'Cool. Suits me. Weeding's a breeze.'

I didn't have time to thank him before the lines marched off in separate directions. Jasper saw me leaving with the other group and her eyes widened. I put my finger to my mouth so she wouldn't say anything. Knowing Jasper, she'd figure it out in a flash anyway.

I'd been right about the kennel — it was the long, white building behind the house. In the distance I could see the caged playground, lying empty and quiet. If only I could find the key, I thought. I'd open it up for all the kids, and lock Auntie Marge and Paddy and Petronella out!

The sound of the dogs barking was loud enough outside the kennel, but inside it was almost deafening. While we waited, I had a quick scout around looking for Scoop. The first thing I noticed was that each dog had its own stall, with a bed of old blankets to sleep on, and two bowls. Everything was spotlessly clean.

I'd never seen so many dogs in my life, except at the pound. No wonder they called this place the Puppy Factory. I ticked off the breeds as I passed them:

German shepherd, silky terrier, Rhodesian ridgeback, labrador . . . the list went on. It seemed like every type of dog in the world was here — except for plain old mongrel. Looked like old Marge and Pegleg Paddy had expensive taste in pets.

I counted them under my breath as I passed the stalls. I was up to number twenty-eight when I spotted Scoop, standing up with his paws against the wire with his tail wagging and his tongue hanging out.

'Scoop!' I opened the wire gate and almost fell over as Scoop threw himself at me, licking my face and yelping with excitement. There was no doubt about it — he remembered me!

'Hey, what are you doing?' It was one of the other boys, Hamish. He looked friendly enough, but I wasn't ready to trust anyone just yet. 'That dog looks like he knows you!'

I shrugged and cuddled Scoop closer. 'Hello again, fella,' I whispered, taking him back with me to join the group.

'Why did you swap places with Tyson before?' Hamish was still looking at me curiously, waiting for an answer. He was a big boy about my age, with an open, honest kind of face.

'Oh, I just like dogs,' I said. That was true enough. I tucked Scoop under one arm and stuck out my hand. 'My name's Hugo.'

Hamish grabbed it and shook it vigorously. 'Pleased to meet you Hugo! Welcome to the un-Fun Prison Camp. How long are you in for?'

'One week.' I noticed Hamish had traces of black paint on his hands. He must have been the one who changed the sign at the front gate. I decided that I liked him, but I wasn't about to tell him my escape plan.

'Half your luck. Me and Lucy-Kate — she's my sister — are here for two whole weeks. Mum and Dad dropped us off three days before the holidays started. They had to go to Queensland to look after my sick grandma.'

'They promithed uth we'd like it,' lisped his little sister, her bottom lip trembling. 'But we don't.'

Before too long, I'd met the other kids in the group too. All of them hated being at Auntie Marge's as much as I did.

'She's an old battleaxe,' said Emily fiercely. 'Mum and Dad thought I'd spend all my time playing — but Marge treats us like slaves!'

'The problem is that she's such a good liar,' added Robert. He was the dark-haired boy who had served us the porridge. 'This is the second time I've been here. Every time my mum rings up to check on me, Auntie Marge sweet-talks her. She just won't believe how awful it is.'

I stroked Scoop's silky-smooth black head and thought for a moment. Surely it wouldn't hurt to tell them about *Street Wise*. In fact, it would probably help me to get more information if the other kids knew I was writing a story. Maybe they'd even help me.

'I think I know a way we can get the grown-ups to believe us,' I said. 'But I have to swear you to secrecy. If Auntie Marge finds out what I'm up to, it'll blow the whole thing.'

Quickly, I told them about our newspaper. How the three of us — Jasper, Toby and I — had started *Street Wise* because nobody else was standing up for kids' rights. Then how Frankie had joined us as our photographer and become my best friend into the bargain. I told them about all the stories we'd covered — how we'd saved our local park from a big developer, and how we'd interviewed one of the world's most famous pop stars, Mandy Miami, after tracking her down through the Internet.

At first, they thought I was making it all up. But as I explained how we put the newspaper together on Toby's computer, I could see that, one by one, they were starting to believe me.

'So, let's get this straight,' said Hamish. 'You're a reporter, and you reckon you can write the real story about Auntie Marge's Fun Camp for your newspaper?'

I nodded. 'But I need facts. Details. I'm convinced there's something funny going on here — but I need as much information as possible to prove it. That's how all of you can help. It's the only way we can get our parents to believe us.'

Emily clapped her hands. 'Maybe they'll even shut it down, so we'd never have to come here again!'

Hamish's eyes lit up. 'Sounds good to me!' He looked around at the others. 'I say we help Hugo as much as we can. Does everyone agree?'

They all nodded. A wave of exhilaration swept over me. Things were going even better than I expected! Having the other kids on my side made the job a lot easier. The first thing I needed to know was the location of the phone and the computer, so I could contact Toby . . .

But before I had a chance to ask, something happened that made Scoop prick up his ears and sit up stiffly in my arms. The sound of footsteps, walking towards the kennel. But these were no ordinary footsteps.

CLUMP-clump. CLUMP-clump. CLUMP-clump. One heavy footstep, one light. Instantly, the other kids froze.

'It's Pegleg Paddy!' Robert turned pale. 'Quick, into line everybody! If he catches us talking we're history!'

I remembered what Tyson had told us about Pegleg Paddy: '*As rough as guts and mean as a feral pig.*' Until now, I'd only seen him from a distance — but it looked like that was about to change.

CLUMP-clump. CLUMP-clump. The footsteps drew closer.

'Hugo, the dog!' Hamish gestured frantically at Scoop. 'Nobody's allowed to handle the dogs until Paddy says so. If he sees him out of his box, he'll go berserk! Get rid of him, quickly.'

I looked around desperately. I was too far away from Scoop's kennel to put him back. I didn't want to risk putting him in with another dog in case they started fighting. And there was no way I was just going to dump him on the ground. Scoop was my responsibility now. If anyone was going to be punished, it should be me — not him.

CLUMP-clump. A tall, dark shadow fell across the doorway. I glanced down at Scoop and gave him a final hug. There was nothing I could do. Pegleg Paddy was going to catch me red-handed.

Suddenly, a hand reached out of nowhere and plucked Scoop out of my arms.

'Hey . . .!'

A low, soft voice whispered in my ear. 'Get in line, and stay quiet. I'll take care of the dog.'

I spun around. It was a girl I hadn't seen before. A girl with snow white hair.

Chapter Six

'What's that mutt doing out of its box?'

It sounded more like a growl than a human voice. Hiding behind Hamish, who was a bit bigger than me, I peeked over his shoulder. Standing there was one of the biggest men I'd ever seen — Pegleg Paddy himself.

Up close, he looked even more scary. His black wrap-around sunglasses were like a sinister mask and a silver hoop dangled from one ear. The bottom half of his face was covered by a bushy beard and moustache. But strangely enough, his head was completely bald. I looked closer. It was shaved as smooth as a billiard ball.

He wore a faded denim jacket over a black T-shirt, which had a picture of a grinning skeleton riding a motorbike, and the words, SWAMP ZOMBIES written on it. Trying not to look too obvious, I checked out his legs. One of them, I knew, was wooden. That's why they called him Pegleg. He was wearing jeans, so I couldn't really tell the difference until I reached the bottom. On one foot, he wore a brown leather boot. But where the other foot should have been, there was nothing at all — just a smooth, polished wooden stump.

'He's only a pup. He was pining for his mother.' The girl's voice was calm and strong and her sad grey eyes looked unflinchingly at Pegleg Paddy. She didn't seem scared of him at all. Maybe because she was older than us — by my guess, about fourteen. I noticed that she was fiddling with a gold locket around her neck. 'If he doesn't get some affection, he'll become sick, and then he's no good to you at all.'

I looked at the girl admiringly. It would have taken me hours to come up with an excuse like that. She cradled Scoop in her arms and stared defiantly at Paddy.

'Hmmph!' He grunted, then turned Scoop's head towards him and peered into his eyes. 'You're too soft on these mongrels, Flossie. He looks all right to me.'

Flossie! This must be the Flossie Fleabags that Tyson had talked about! I took another look at her. She seemed too pretty to have a name like that. I remembered what Tyson had said: 'Flossie Fleabags . . . she's the only guardian angel around here.'

With her snow white hair, she did look a bit like an angel. Except that angels don't look sad — and they don't wear ragged clothes that they've obviously grown out of. The dress Flossie was wearing was old and patched, and it looked too small for her. She had a shabby pink cardigan over the top of it and a pair of dirty white runners on her feet. Apart from the gold locket, it was the sort of outfit Cinderella's poor cousin would wear.

'If he looks all right it's because he's had a bit of TLC — tender loving care,' said Flossie sharply. 'No thanks to you.'

I held my breath. Did anybody speak to Pegleg Paddy like that and survive?

But Pegleg didn't seem to notice. He just shrugged and turned away.

'He won't be here much longer anyway,' he said gruffly. 'I've had some interest in him already.' He clumped off stiffly, throwing one last remark over his shoulder. 'And another thing, make sure the border collie's washed and combed last thing before teatime. I'm doing a delivery at nine o'clock tonight.'

My heart skipped a beat. What did he mean, that Scoop wouldn't be here much longer? It sounded like Pegleg was taking the border collie away tonight — maybe Scoop was next on the list!

My mind buzzed with questions. What was the point of bringing these dogs here, only to take them away again? I thought they were pets — but Pegleg didn't treat them like pets. He didn't even have names for them. It just didn't make sense.

I started to panic. I'd already said goodbye to Scoop once — when Dad took him to the pound. Now that we had been magically brought back together, there was no way I was letting him go again. As I watched Pegleg Paddy leave, I made up my mind. If Jasper and I were going to escape, Scoop was coming with us!

Scoop whimpered and struggled to get out of Flossie's arms. She checked that Pegleg Paddy was out of sight, then handed him back to me.

'You two seem like good friends,' she said reassuringly. 'Here, why don't you look after him for today?'

As the other kids gathered around, I took Scoop gratefully.

'You were brave, Flothie,' said Lucy-Kate, tugging at Flossie's dress. 'He'th horrible!'

Flossie laughed — a bright, tinkling sound like wind chimes. 'Oh, Pegleg's just full of bluster and bad manners,' she said. 'His bark's much worse than his bite. Which reminds me, these dogs need looking after! Let's get to work.'

With Scoop at my ankles, and Flossie in charge, I started to feel a lot happier. Now that Pegleg was out of sight, everybody relaxed. They all seemed to know what to do and quickly set about doing their allotted tasks. With so many dogs to feed, water, wash and walk, I could see how we'd be busy most of the day.

Flossie noticed me standing alone in the middle of the kennels, and came over with a smile.

'You're on walking duty, aren't you Hugo?'

I nodded. 'How do you know my name?'

Flossie laughed again. 'Oh, I know most of what goes on here. You've got a sister, too, haven't you? I saw you arrive with your mum and dad.' She suddenly went quiet, and I saw that she was touching the gold locket again.

I was still trying to figure out how Flossie fitted in at the Fun Camp. She was so nice! Not at all like Auntie Marge, Pegleg and Petronella. And yet she'd obviously been here for a long time. Did she just work here or was this her home?

'Is Pegleg Paddy your dad?' I blurted out. 'And is Auntie Marge your grandma? Is that why you live here?'

Flossie looked taken aback. Then she grimaced, and shook her head. 'Not on your life! I'm not related to either of them, thank goodness.' She gently opened the locket. 'Look. These are my parents.'

Inside the locket there were two tiny photographs. One showed a dark-haired woman with a soft, sweet smile. The other was a man with serious eyes, and the same snow white hair as Flossie.

'Where are they?'

Flossie hesitated. 'In Africa. They're zoologists. I'm going to be one too, when I grow up.' She snapped the locket shut and tucked it into her dress. I got the feeling the subject was closed.

'Was it you who brought us the food last night?' I asked curiously. 'And rang the doorbell to distract Auntie Marge?'

Flossie threw back her head and laughed her soft, tinkling laugh again. 'So many questions! I heard you telling the kids you're a reporter — and now I believe it!' She beckoned me to follow her. 'Come and I'll give you a leash to walk the dogs with. Don't let them off the leash or they'll run off and you'll spend all day chasing them. Take them one at a time, thirty-five minutes each.'

'But it *was* you, wasn't it?' I persisted. 'Why are you so nice to us?'

Flossie's sad grey eyes looked deep into mine as she handed me the leash.

'Let's just say I know how lonely it is not to have your mum and dad around,' she said. 'When I can, I help.'

As I led the border collie out the door I looked back and saw her, still holding the gold locket and staring sadly into space.

'She's an orphan,' declared Hamish, holding onto the leash with both hands as the big German shepherd tried to break into a gallop. 'Her real name's Flora Hamilton. Paddy calls her Flossie Fleabags because she lives in a little room off the kennels.'

I waited while the border collie sniffed its two-hundredth tree trunk. Scoop was chasing birds, rushing back every few seconds to check on me.

'So, why is she here?' I asked.

'Her parents brought her here eight months ago. Then they went overseas and never came back for her.' Hamish shook his head regretfully. 'Auntie Marge says it's because they didn't want her, but Flossie says that's not true. She's convinced they're going to turn up one day.'

My heart ached as I thought of poor Flossie, waiting and waiting for the parents who never came back for her. Then, a horrifying thought struck me.

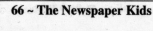

What if that happened with *our* parents? What if Mum and Dad never came back for us and we were stuck at Auntie Marge's forever?

'It suits Auntie Marge because she's got a full-time servant,' Hamish continued. 'Flossie's a great cook, and she's much better with the dogs than Paddy is. And she does the accounts in the office after she's finished work each day.'

My ears pricked up. I forgot about Mum and Dad for the moment as I digested this important piece of information. Something had just clicked inside my brain. *'When I can, I help,'* Flossie had told me. If Flossie worked in the office, chances are she could help me get to the computer . . .

I crept down the stairs towards the girls' dormitory.

'Pssst. Jasper. It's me.'

I jumped as a ghostly apparition appeared silently at the door. It was Jasper in her nightie.

'Shhh! You'll wake Petronella! What took you so long?' she grumbled.

The old house lay dark and silent, except for the sound of the television coming from one of the rooms. Flattening myself against the wall, I peered cautiously around the doorway. Auntie Marge and Pegleg Paddy were sitting with their backs to us, watching a comedy show.

I gave Jasper the thumbs up sign, and we tiptoed past them without a sound.

Flossie had left the office door unlocked, just as she'd promised. We slipped inside and closed the door behind us. By the soft light of a desk lamp, I could see what we'd come for — the computer. It looked strangely out of place among all the old furniture.

'Look, it's got a modem!' Jasper whispered jubilantly. 'You were right, Hugo — they're on the Internet!'

I heaved a sigh of relief. That was one problem solved. Talking on the phone was too risky — we'd be heard for sure. Besides, at this time of night Toby was always in the Cave — the old shed in his backyard which we'd made into our newspaper office. I could see him now — hunched over the computer, peering at it through his thick spectacles and trying to come up with the world's cleverest headline. Well, he was about to get the shock of his life.

Moving quickly and quietly, I turned the computer on and accessed the E-mail function.

'Hurry up,' urged Jasper, glancing nervously at the door.

Now that I had the chance to talk to Toby, I couldn't think what to say. There was so much to tell him, I didn't know where to start. First of all, I had to make sure he was there.

> Are you there, Toby? This is urgent — Hugo.

I zapped off the shortest E-mail I could think of and waited.

'He's not there,' groaned Jasper after three seconds. 'I knew it.'

'Give him a chance.' I stared at the computer, willing it to give me a response.

BEEP! The E-mail icon was flashing. A reply!

> What's up?

That was Toby all right — short and to the point.

'You're taking forever, Hugo.' Jasper pushed me off the chair impatiently and sat herself down. 'Let me do it. After all, Toby is *my* best friend.'

Her long fingers flew over the keyboard.

> Hi, it's me, Jasper. I've just spent the whole day scrubbing toilets. Fun Camp is no fun at all. We're being held prisoner. Kids' rights non-existent. Have enough information for a brilliant story but need your help to escape. Camp is surrounded by electric fence with security cameras. Any ideas?

I had to admit, she'd summed it up perfectly. There was a long pause. Knowing Toby, he'd be pacing the Cave weighing up all the possibilities very carefully. Toby's a genius but he never makes a quick decision.

After what seemed an eternity, the E-mail icon beeped again.

> I'm holding the front page. Great story but situation seems dangerous. Don't, repeat don't, try to leave on foot. Suggest stow away. Think Bonzo!

I knew what Toby meant straight away. *Bonzo's Big Break* was one of our favourite books. In it, Bonzo breaks out of jail by hiding in a laundry truck.

'How are we supposed to hide in a laundry truck when Auntie Marge gets the kids to do all the laundry here?' Jasper frowned.

I grabbed her arm excitedly. 'It doesn't have to be a laundry truck, silly! It can be any car or truck that comes in and out of this place. Someone that Auntie Marge would open the electric gate for without even thinking.'

I typed a reply to Toby.

> Brilliant idea! Will be catching the Bonzo Express the next time it leaves.
>
> PS Tell Frankie we've found Scoop!

Jasper raised an eyebrow. 'The *Bonzo Express*? What are you talking about?'

I checked my watch. 8.45 pm. *'I'm making a delivery at nine o'clock tonight,'* Pegleg Paddy had said.

There was no time to lose. The Bonzo Express was leaving in fifteen minutes — and Jasper, Scoop and I were going to be on it!

Chapter Seven

The ghostly light of the moon shone down on Pegleg Paddy's rusty red jeep.

I gave Jasper a leg-up into the back of it and threw an old blanket over her.

'Hey, it's cold under here,' came the muffled cry. 'I'm sitting on metal.'

I scrabbled around in the back of the jeep and tossed her a hessian sack from a pile in the corner. It was the same sort Paddy used to carry the puppies in.

'Here, sit on this. And don't move. I'll be back in a minute.'

'Ouch! Something's giving me itchy bites,' complained Jasper from underneath the blanket.

'Well, scratch them. I'm going to get Scoop.'

I glanced at my watch as I sped over to the kennel. 8.50 pm. I had ten minutes to pick up Scoop and get back to the jeep without Pegleg catching me. That should give me just enough time to say goodbye to Flossie.

The kennels were in darkness, except for a yellow glow of light coming from a window at the far end. That must be Flossie's room. I crept up to the window and peeked in, just to make sure.

Flossie was in there, poring over a pile of books by the light of two candles. She was wearing glasses, and her snow white hair was pulled back neatly into a ponytail. Good. She was awake.

The door was on the other side, opposite the window. As I crept around the outside of the kennels to reach it, I stumbled over something in the darkness.

At first, I thought it was a pile of old belts. I could see the buckles and some other shiny bits glinting in the moonlight. Curious, I picked up one of the objects I'd tripped over. It was too short to be a belt. I peered more closely at it, and saw it was a dog collar, with a registration tag and a silver name plate on it. There was a name engraved on it, but it was too dark to read.

No wonder I'd almost fallen flat on my face. There must have been dozens of dog collars in the pile — hundreds, even. So why weren't the dogs wearing them? The collars had obviously been discarded — tossed outside the kennels and left to rot in the rain and the sun.

I threw the collar back on the pile and walked on. There was no time to think about it now. The best I could do was add it to the list of unsolved mysteries about Auntie Marge's Fun Camp and forget about it. With any luck, I'd only be here for a few more minutes.

I knocked on Flossie's door quietly, then without waiting for a reply, opened it and slipped inside.

'Hugo!' Flossie took off her glasses and stared at me in surprise. 'What are you doing here?'

'I've come to say goodbye.'

Quickly, I filled her in on the plan — how Jasper and I were going to escape in the back of Pegleg's ute, then write a story that would expose the truth about Auntie Marge's so-called Fun Camp.

'Once the grown-ups read it, they might even close the camp down forever!' I finished excitedly. I looked at Flossie, expecting her to be as enthusiastic as I was. Instead, she just slowly put her glasses back on and went back to reading her book without a word.

'Flossie?' I asked hesitantly. 'Don't you think it's a good plan?'

Flossie took a deep breath and raised her eyes to me. She looked troubled.

'If the camp closes down, what will happen to me?' She gestured around her room. 'I know it's not much, but this is the only home I've got . . . now.' One fine, pale hand fluttered up to touch the locket. I knew she was thinking about her parents.

'But you can't stay here forever,' I said. 'Auntie Marge and Paddy — they're nasty people.'

Flossie patted the pile of books. 'No, I don't plan on staying forever, Hugo. Just as long as it takes me to get into university so I can become a zoologist, like my mother and father.' Her voice broke.

'Don't cry, Flossie.' I patted her shoulder, trying to comfort her. 'I know they'll come back for you one day. Maybe they got lost in Africa . . .' My voice faded away.

Flossie dried her eyes with a small, blue hanky. 'That's what I think, too, Hugo. If I tell you a secret, will you promise not to tell anyone?'

I nodded. That's something you have to do when you're a reporter — learn to keep your mouth shut. Otherwise, people stop telling you things.

'When I become a zoologist, I'm going to Africa to look for them.' Flossie sighed deeply, then sat down at her books again. 'That's the plan, anyway.'

I stared at Flossie's locket. An idea was starting to form in my brain . . .

I glanced at my watch. 8.57 pm.

'Flossie, give me the photos out of your locket. Hurry!'

Flossie looked at me like I'd gone troppo.

'Are you nuts, Hugo? These are more precious to me than . . . than anything! They're all I've got left . . .'

'Flossie, listen to me,' I said urgently. 'You don't have to wait until you go to university to find your parents. Give me the photos and we'll publish them in *Street Wise*. We'll write a story about you, and I bet you anything someone will help us track your parents down!'

Slowly, Flossie opened the locket and pulled out the miniature photos. She gazed at them adoringly. 'Are you sure you won't lose them?' she pleaded, with tears in her eyes.

'Cross my heart.' I grabbed the photos and bolted out the door.

'This blanket stinks,' grumbled Jasper, as the ute rattled along. 'Trust you to find the world's smelliest old rag to hide under. And I'm sure it's got fleas.'

'Sorry, it's the best I could do at short notice,' I told her cheerfully. 'Next time, I'll make sure the limousine is equipped to Madam's standards.'

Cautiously, I threw the corner of the blanket back, making sure I kept my head down. The last thing we needed was for Pegleg Paddy to see us in his rear-vision mirror.

Scoop lifted his nose into the cold night air and yelped joyously.

'Shhh!' I cuddled Scoop closer, trying to calm him down. 'Not long now, little fella. Soon we'll be out of this place — and you'll have a real home.'

The border collie flopped down next to us, her tail wagging. Thanks to our walk today, she already knew me. So when Pegleg loaded her into the jeep, the collie simply gave the old pile of blankets in the corner a friendly sniff, before finding herself a spot to lie down. Lucky for us, Pegleg never imagined that the old pile of blankets concealed three escapees — two human, one canine.

Jasper poked her head out from under the blanket and drew in big lungfuls of fresh air. The old jeep clattered and bounced along until we could both hear our teeth chattering.

The jeep was going so quickly that before we knew it, we'd reached the big front gate. Carefully, I inched my head over the side of the ute for a last look at the camp. Paddy stopped the ute, and beeped the horn impatiently. Seconds later, the iron gate slid silently open — and we were outside.

'Freedom!' Jasper pinched me jubilantly as the jeep drove off noisily. We watched the sign saying 'Auntie Marge's Fun Camp' get smaller and smaller until it finally disappeared. 'Let's jump out as soon as he slows down.'

I shook my head. 'Don't be silly. We're miles from anywhere. And we might hurt ourselves. We'll just have to wait until he stops.'

To pass the time, I started thinking about tomorrow morning, when Chief Dobber Duff was going to find our beds empty. What a shock she would get! I could just imagine Auntie Marge's angry face when Petronella broke the news to her. Well, it would be too late to catch us then. We'd be at Toby's place writing our story ... except that it was Scoop I could see sitting at Toby's desk, chewing on a pen and telling us to go and fetch a stick for him ...

'Hugo! Hugo, wake up! We're there!'

With a start, I realised I'd dropped off to sleep. 'What . . .?'

'Shhh.' Jasper threw the blanket back over our heads as the car door slammed. 'Keep still.'

Under the blanket it was pitch black. All I could hear was Jasper's nose whistling slightly as she breathed, and the unmistakeable sound of Pegleg Paddy's footsteps.

'Paddy! Is that you?'

It was a voice I didn't recognise. Scoop's ears pricked up. I laid my hand gently on his head, and he seemed to understand: not a sound.

'G'day, Merv.' Peeking through a tiny slit in the blanket, I saw Pegleg unbolt the back of the jeep and shoo the collie out. 'I've got the dog. Young female border collie, suitable for breeding, just like you ordered.'

'Good stuff.' The other voice sounded pleased. 'I've got a couple of buyers willing to pay three hundred dollars for her.'

Three hundred dollars! My eyes popped. That was more pocket money than I'd earn in a million years.

'Just make sure you check them out,' said Paddy gruffly. 'I don't want any undercover cops busting our little enterprise.'

I nudged Jasper. It sounded like Pegleg Paddy was involved in something illegal — something to do with his dogs.

The other man laughed nastily. 'No worries about that. We've got 'em fooled all right. The local papers are calling us the Phantom Dog-nappers — but they haven't got a clue it's us.'

The Phantom Dog-nappers . . . where had I heard that before? Of course! The *Blue Rock Bugle* had done a story about them a few months earlier.

'You and Marge have had dogs for so many years,' continued the man, 'who would ever suspect it's you?'

My mind was racing. So Pegleg Paddy was selling pedigree dogs that he either stole — or picked up at the pound, like Scoop. That explained why he kept coming and going with dogs. That was why his dogs were all pedigree breeds worth hundreds of dollars each. That was why he didn't give any of them names — he sold them.

Suddenly, it was all falling into place. Pegleg Paddy was one of the Phantom Dog-nappers. What a story!

Jasper nudged me. 'Come on, here's our chance,' she whispered. 'We can slip out now while they're talking. If we can find a phone box, we can ring Toby reverse charges.'

Jasper was right — but something made me hesitate. In the last thirty seconds, the story had become much bigger than I ever imagined. It was no longer just about Auntie Marge's Hell Camp. It was about a stolen dog racket that the police were trying to crack.

But I had enough experience as a reporter to know there was one vital thing missing. Hard evidence.

'Don't move,' I told Jasper. 'We're going back in. Back to the camp.'

When I knocked on Flossie's door, she couldn't believe it was me.

'But I saw you leave ... I saw you get into the jeep ...'

As I explained what I had heard that evening, Flossie's grey eyes widened. 'I knew Pegleg was up to something dodgy, but I never imagined he was a criminal.'

Then her face fell. 'I suppose that means you can't put my parents' pictures in your paper.'

'In a few more days I can,' I assured her. 'But I need to gather more evidence for my story. Otherwise, nobody will believe it.'

Flossie nodded, but I could tell she was disappointed.

As I made my way back to the house, a thousand thoughts jostled for attention inside my head. Before I went to bed, I had to access the Internet and contact Toby, telling him the new developments. I also had to record in my notebook the conversation I had heard between Pegleg

Paddy and the other man, before I forgot any of it.

And I had to do something to help Flossie. I took the two tiny photographs out of my pocket and studied them in the moonlight. Maybe there *was* something I could do straight away . . .

Chapter Eight

I didn't sleep much that night. I was too busy going over my story, writing and rewriting it in my head, and trying to piece together all the bits of the puzzle. If only Toby and Frankie were here! My own brain wasn't big enough to solve a mystery like this. Even Jasper's wasn't a lot of help. It needed all four brains working together.

I tossed and turned, replaying the night's conversation in my mind. By the sound of it, Pegleg was stealing pedigree dogs and passing them on to a middle-man, who then sold them to people for hundreds of dollars. But how could I prove it?

'Find the trail,' Toby's E-mail had said. 'Crooks always leave a trail . . .'

Tomorrow, I thought fuzzily, as my tired brain drifted off to sleep. Tomorrow morning, I'll slip away from the others and do a bit of snooping around . . .

But as it turned out, I didn't get the chance.

'Everyone over to the playground — now!' yelled Petronella. She gave two shrill blasts on her whistle. 'MOVE IT!'

'You beaut!' said Tyson. He was on dog-washing duty with me. 'Must be some new kids arriving. Now we get to play for a bit.'

A giant yawn nearly split my head in two. Thanks to my adventure the night before, everything I did felt like it was in slow motion. I'd even dozed off in the middle of washing a big rottweiler, and woken up to find him washing me — by licking my face!

'Here, leave the dogs with me,' said Flossie, walking over to us. 'I'll mind Scoop. Go and enjoy yourselves in the playground — you mightn't get another chance before you go home.'

She didn't have to tell us twice. Jumping and whooping with excitement, the kids on kennel duty ran to join the others outside the playground. Jasper, who was rostered on kitchen detail, was talking to Lucy-Kate and pretended not to see me. She wasn't speaking to me after I made her come back to Auntie Marge's with me instead of going straight to the police with our story. My ears were still burning after the scolding she'd given me in the ute on the way back. I shrugged. She'd get over it. The fact was, we needed proof — and I was determined to find it.

'Everybody line up, and stop talking,' ordered Petronella, rattling her bunch of keys. 'Otherwise I won't open the gate.'

Boy, what a bossy-boots. She acted like she was the most important person in the world just because she had the key to the playground.

'But Petronella, if you don't open the gate, we'll have to go back to work, and then it would look like we're not enjoying ourselves,' said Jasper innocently. 'And I don't think Auntie Marge would like that . . . do you?'

Petronella scowled and threw open the gate.

'Just get in there and start playing,' she barked. 'And make sure you look like you're having FUN!' She gave a final blast on her whistle, locked the gate behind us and stomped off.

'Yes, sir!' Tyson gave Petronella's departing back a snappy salute. 'Come on, Hugo — race you to the slide!'

The next few minutes were the best time I'd had since I got to Auntie Marge's. In fact, I almost forgot we were prisoners. Without Petronella spying on us, it was almost like being back in the real world.

'Hey! Come and see the new recruits,' suggested Tyson. He jumped off the monkey-bars and ran over to the wire enclosure. I followed reluctantly. We'd meet the new kids soon enough. Why waste precious playing time gawking at them from a distance?

'Look. The dad's got a new four-wheel drive.' Tyson pointed to a shiny blue Adventurer. I stared at it morosely. It was exactly like the one Toby's dad had bought recently. Just what I needed — another reminder of home.

'There's two of them. Boy and a girl. Boy's older, I'd say,' reported Tyson, peering out through the wire. He started yelling: 'HEY VICTIMS! Get out now while you can! You have been warned! Turn back from the gates of hell or be forever DOOMED!'

He turned to me and grinned. 'See? I try to warn people but nobody believes me!'

I watched as the figure of Auntie Marge bustled over to the big blue car, wiping her hands on her apron. Aha, I thought. The old 'I've just been baking biscuits' trick. A tall, thin man with legs as long as bean-stalks emerged from the driver's side and shook her hand. That must be the father.

'Go home, thuckerth!' shrilled Lucy-Kate from the boat-swing. 'You'll hate it here!'

'Auntie Marge is a rotten old pig!' shouted Jasper, getting into the spirit of things.

'Pig! Pig! Pig! Auntie Marge is a rotten old pig!' chanted the others.

The boy and girl stopped talking to each other and looked over at the playground. Probably, I thought, they were wondering what all the noise was about — just as Jasper and I had. The boy's glasses flashed in the sunlight, and I saw him raise his hand to push them more firmly onto the bridge of his nose.

I gasped. There was only one person I knew in the whole world who pushed his glasses onto the bridge of his nose *exactly like that*. Only one person whose glasses were too big for him and were always slipping off.

I pushed my face against the wire and strained my eyes, hardly daring to hope.

There was no doubt about it. The boy with the glasses was Toby. And the girl standing next to him, with the short dark hair and brown skin, was none other than my best friend, Frankie Halliday.

'Are you sure it was them?' Jasper whispered as Petronella herded us out of the playground. She still wasn't being too friendly but at least she was talking to me again.

The blue Adventurer had driven off and the two new recruits were nowhere to be seen.

'Positive,' I replied. 'My guess is they're posing as brother and sister. Toby must have let his dad in on the secret.' Mr Trotter was a reporter for the *Blue Rock Bugle*, and the only grown-up who was ever allowed into the Cave.

'I doubt it,' scoffed Jasper. 'The last thing Toby would want is the *Bugle* to scoop the story.'

'You two, stop gas-bagging!' snapped Petronella. 'We're already behind as it is, thanks to this interruption. You'll all have to work twice as hard now to make up for it.'

As we split up to march back to our work stations, I gave Jasper our secret 'thumbs up' sign. I even had to stop myself from leaping in the air with excitement. Now that Toby and Frankie were here, we'd wrap this story up in no time. With Toby's brains, and Frankie's photographs, the newspaper kids would crack this case and be out of here before Auntie Marge even noticed.

That's what I thought, anyway. Pity I didn't have my fortune-telling crystal ball with me . . .

By the time I saw Frankie and Toby again — at the dinner table — I was bursting to talk to them. It was

bad enough waiting the whole day to see them —
now we were trapped under Petronella's eagle eye,
and forbidden to speak.

Hamish saw my dilemma. 'Let the newspaper kids
sit together,' he told the others quietly. I'd confided
in him earlier that day and, like me, he thought it
best the four of us didn't let on to Marge and Pegleg
that we were friends. 'And remember — not a word
to Petronella,' I'd said.

The message spread like magic, and before too
long Frankie, Toby and I were sitting side by side,
nudging each other with excitement. Jasper, who
was doling out the baked beans and Brussels
sprouts, caught my eye and grinned broadly. I
could tell she was as happy as I was to have the
team back together — even if we couldn't talk to
each other.

I saw Hamish glance at us, then whisper
something to Lucy-Kate. The next thing I knew,
Lucy-Kate was having a giant attack of the hiccups.

'What's wrong with you?' demanded Petronella
rudely, her mouth full of half-chewed Brussels
sprouts.

'HIC!' replied Lucy-Kate. The next hiccup was so
violent she nearly fell off her chair. 'HIC!'

'It's the hiccups, Petronella,' Hamish informed her.

'I know it's hiccups, you idiot! Tell her to stop.'

Hamish shook his head gravely. 'You don't understand. If she gets the hiccups really badly, it can trigger an asthma attack.'

Right on cue, Lucy-Kate gave an impressive wheeze, followed by another hiccup.

'Yep — definitely a case of fatal hiccups,' said Hamish. He caught my eye and winked. I twigged — the whole thing was a trick. Good old Hamish! 'If she doesn't lie down, she'll stop breathing and die. Mum and Dad would be really cross,' he added.

Petronella looked alarmed. The way Lucy-Kate was performing, you'd think she was about to cark it any second. 'Well, I don't want to get into trouble. Come on, you silly girl — I'll take you up to the dormitory.'

With Petronella out of the way, we finally got to talk. Toby told us how — like me — he'd tossed and turned all night after our conversation on the Internet. That morning, he'd been hit by a brainwave — he and Frankie, masquerading as brother and sister, would come to the camp to join us.

It wasn't hard to convince their parents. They just told them the four of us were missing each other, and we wanted to be together at the Fun Camp. That was true enough!

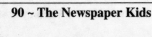

'I've got all my cameras hidden in my bag,' said Frankie excitedly. 'If what you're saying is true — if this Pegleg fellow really is a criminal — you'll need photographs to prove it.'

'Oh, it's true all right,' I reassured her. 'Pegleg Paddy is as crooked as a dog's hind leg.'

Toby stared at me impassively through his thick glasses. 'How do you know that, Hugo?'

'Of course I know it!' I spluttered angrily. 'I told you — Jasper and I heard him selling that collie. We heard the other man admit they were Phantom Dog-nappers! Don't you believe me?'

Toby patted me on the back. 'Relax, Hugo. Of course *I* believe you — but you need proof. You can't just write a story based on what you've heard. Do you know this other man's name, for example, or where he lives?'

I shook my head numbly.

'Well, how about the dogs? Do you know where they come from? Who their real owners are?'

Again, I shook my head. I knew what Toby was getting at. If we printed my story without proof, it would be my word against Pegleg's. He could simply deny everything — and then *we'd* be the ones in trouble. People would think we were making the whole thing up.

I banged my fist on the table in frustration. 'It's so

unfair! I know Pegleg's a crook, but he doesn't leave a trail. The dogs don't have names, they don't even have collars . . .'

I stopped. Collars . . . where had I seen dog collars?

'What is it, Hugo?' Frankie shook me. 'Is something wrong?'

The kitchen door flew open as Petronella walked back in. She saw us huddled together and her eyes narrowed.

'Meet me at the south end of the kennels tomorrow morning at ten o'clock,' I said urgently in a low voice. 'All of us have to sneak away from our jobs. There's something I want to show you . . .'

'This is amazing.' Toby picked up a handful of collars and read out the names on them. 'Tootsie. Rembrandt. Spot — gee, that's an original name,' he joked. 'I wonder what sort of dogs they are?'

'I think it's sad.' Frankie focussed her camera on the pile of collars, and snapped another picture. 'Just think. Hundreds of poor little pets, stolen from their families, and their new owners don't even know their real name. Hold a collar up for me, Jasper. I want a close-up.'

Jasper sifted through the pile and held up a black collar with studs on it. 'I bet this belonged to a big

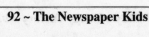

rottie, or a German shepherd. It says Rex. And look, it's got a phone number too.'

Most of them did. As I rummaged through the pile with Scoop helping me, I thought of all those owners, waiting anxiously by the telephone for somebody to ring and say, 'We've found your dog!' But of course, nobody would have rung, because the dogs weren't lost. They'd been stolen — by the Phantom Dog-nappers.

Scoop dragged another collar out of the pile, and shook it from side to side as though it were a rat. I stroked his black silky ears. Thank goodness *he* didn't have another owner somewhere. Pegleg Paddy must have picked him up at the pound after Dad left him there. And when I first found him on the way home from school, he wasn't wearing a collar. So there was no doubt in my mind — or in Scoop's — that I was his real owner. We just had to convince Mum and Dad of that.

Toby stood up and dusted his hands. 'Well, I think these collars are the proof we need that Pegleg Paddy is running a stolen dog racket. They're a good start, anyway.'

'All I need now is some photos of the dogs themselves,' added Frankie happily, snapping away.

'Then we can contact the dogs' owners and the police — and it's all over red rover!' Jasper punched the air triumphantly. 'How's that for a front page newspaper story?'

'*And* I'm going to make sure we keep Scoop,' I declared, picking him up. 'As the official *Street Wise* mascot!'

Just then, I saw a movement out of the corner of my eye. Somebody stepped out from behind the kennels.

'Not so fast, newshounds,' said a familiar voice.

It was Petronella. She'd heard the whole thing.

Chapter Nine

Nobody said a single word. 'Hand over the camera,' Petronella barked. 'Now!'

She glared at Frankie and held out her hand.

V-e-r-y slowly and v-e-r-y carefully, I eased the collar out of Scoop's mouth and slipped it into my pocket.

'You can't have the camera,' replied Frankie calmly. 'It was my father's. It never leaves me.'

Petronella flushed.

'Well, give me the film, then.'

My heart sank. What a disaster! The film would be ruined if Frankie took it out of her camera now. And once Marge and Pegleg knew our plan, the first thing they'd do was get rid of the incriminating evidence. I could see the pile of collars going up in smoke already. No pictures, no proof, *no story*.

'You know, Petronella, there is another way to look at this situation.'

It was Toby. Behind his thick spectacles, his eyes blinked rapidly. It was a sure sign there was some serious brain work going on inside his head.

'Oh really?' sneered Petronella. 'I knew the four of you were up to no good when I saw you at dinner last night — and now I know why.'

Toby nodded. 'I guess being Camp Monitor, you don't miss much.'

Petronella puffed out her chest, and rattled her bunch of keys importantly. 'Too right. I don't miss a thing.'

I caught Jasper's eye and raised my eyebrows. What was Toby up to?

'We should have realised we couldn't fool you — you're much too smart,' agreed Toby. 'In fact, if I'd been half as smart, I would have asked you to help us. Your skills at — er — *surveillance* would have been a real bonus.'

Petronella looked at him suspiciously.

'What do you mean, help you?'

'Well, as you just heard, we run a newspaper. We're always looking for interesting people to interview.' Toby sighed regretfully. 'With your in-depth

knowledge of the camp, you would have been perfect, Petronella. But it looks like we've blown our chances.'

Frankie made a square with her hands and framed Petronella's face with it as though she was looking through a camera lens. 'She's so photogenic, too,' she said.

Petronella's sulky mouth softened a little. 'You'd really put me in your paper?' she asked meekly. 'With a photograph, and everything?' For a moment, she looked almost friendly.

'I can take the photo now, if you like,' offered Frankie. 'Just think how pleased your parents will be!'

I groaned, remembering how Petronella had stormed out of the attic. Frankie didn't realise it, but it was the worst thing she could have said.

At the mention of her parents, a dark cloud crossed Petronella's face. The beginnings of a faint smile immediately turned to an angry scowl.

'My parents are far too busy to read your stupid newspaper!' she yelled. 'And you're probably just lying to me so I won't tell Auntie Marge!'

She grabbed Frankie's camera, wrenched it open and ripped the film out. The four of us watched helplessly as our precious evidence unravelled like reams of black ribbon.

'There!' Petronella turned to us with a nasty smile. 'Now — let's go and explain all this to Auntie Marge. QUICK — MARCH!'

Scoop trotted along at my ankles as Petronella frogmarched us towards the house. My mind was spinning. Our brilliant plan was in tatters. Even Toby's brave attempt to save it had failed. We had been caught red-handed by the camp spy; our evidence destroyed; and now, we were about to be thrown at the mercy of mean old Auntie Marge and her rough-as-guts son.

I grimaced. If Jasper and I had been sent to solitary for something as trivial as a dirty floor, what on earth would the punishment be for this? The torture chamber?

Auntie Marge and Pegleg Paddy were sitting in the television room in front of an electric heater. I smelled liniment and as Petronella pushed us into the room, I saw that Paddy had his trouser leg rolled up to where his knee should have been. His wooden leg was propped up next to the heater. Marge was sprawled in a chair, scoffing a plateful of Flossie's homemade cream cake.

I was so thrilled to see a real wooden leg that I almost forgot to be frightened. I nudged Jasper and pointed to the leg. 'Look. He's taken off his leg,' I whispered. To be honest, I was a little disappointed. It didn't look like a real leg at all — just a bit of polished stick with a cushioned end. I guessed that was where he strapped it on to his stump.

'Whaddya want?' Pegleg put down the liniment bottle and snarled at us.

Scoop's hackles went up, and I heard a soft growl start in his throat.

Auntie Marge shoved the last bit of cream cake into her mouth and wiped her sticky hands on her dress. 'You'd better have a good explanation for this, Petronella.'

I spent the next five minutes — as Petronella spilled the beans — praying the ground would open up and swallow the four of us. She didn't leave a single detail out — she told them everything from how we were going to report them to the police, to how I was planning to keep Scoop as a mascot for the newspaper. Brandishing the ruined film as proof, she pointed to me as the ringleader. As a spy, I had to admit she was first-class. Toby had been right. It was a terrible pity she wasn't on our side.

Pegleg and Auntie Marge listened without a word. Throughout Petronella's long dob-session they stared at me without blinking. The pair of them had eyes like sharks. It wasn't a good feeling.

'You've done well, Petronella,' said Auntie Marge approvingly. Petronella's eyes shone at the praise. 'Now get up to the kennels and build the biggest bonfire you can. I want every one of those collars destroyed. That's the first thing.'

As Petronella ran out of the room, I brushed my hand against my pocket, and felt the outline of the one collar I had managed to save. An idea was forming in my head, but first, we had to get out of this mess we were in.

Auntie Marge turned her cold, shark's eyes back to me. 'And the second thing is deciding what to do with these four . . . TERRORISTS!'

The four of us jumped as she fired the word at us like a bullet.

'Ahem — excuse me,' coughed Toby politely. 'We're not terrorists — we're reporters. Perhaps you'd like to give us *your* side of the story.'

Marge and Pegleg ignored him.

'Give 'em a good thrashin' and lock 'em up in the cellar,' growled Pegleg. 'Without proof nobody's gunna believe 'em, anyway. And they won't get that little black terrier, I'll get rid of 'im tonight. Merv's got a buyer for 'im.'

I watched in horror as he made a lunge for Scoop with his great hairy hands. But before I could push him out of the way, Scoop launched himself through the air and attached himself to Pegleg's hand with his sharp white teeth.

'YOW!' howled Pegleg, trying to shake Scoop off. 'Geddorf me hand, ya mongrel!'

But Scoop hung on gamely, growling ferociously. The more Paddy waved his hand around trying to shake him off, the tighter Scoop hung on. Auntie Marge leapt up, grabbed a broom from behind the door and tried to swat Scoop off Paddy's hand.

'Call your dog off! Call your dog off!' she shrieked at me. 'Shoo, boy! Shoo!'

'Five minutes ago he was *your* dog and *I* was stealing him,' I reminded her. 'Make up your mind, Auntie Marge.'

'HELP!' bellowed Paddy. 'He's chewing my hand off!'

Auntie Marge took a big swing with the broom and whacked as hard as she could.

'Ouch, Ma! You got me on the head! Stop it! Help, somebody! The dog's gone mad!'

Jasper, Toby, Frankie and I watched, speechless with amazement. It was like a cartoon — Auntie Marge, belting Pegleg with a broom; Pegleg, yelling at her to stop and vainly trying to shake Scoop off; and Scoop, growling, hanging on for grim life.

I was wondering how long it would go on for, when suddenly Scoop loosened his hold and dropped to the ground. Paddy gave a relieved cry and started sucking on his wounded hand. 'I'm bleeding, Ma!'

Scoop darted towards the heater, grabbed Paddy's wooden leg, and shot towards the door like a streak of lightning.

'Hey! He's got my leg!' Paddy's anguished cry made Marge freeze with the broom raised above her head.

'Go, boy! *Go!*' I whispered as Scoop rushed past me, Paddy's wooden leg clasped firmly between his teeth. I held my breath, praying that Scoop was smart enough to know that this was one stick he had to take away — not bring back.

I needn't have worried. Scoop must have known we were in trouble — and he knew exactly what to do.

'After him, Ma!' Paddy said.

Auntie Marge shoved us out of the way, and charged after Scoop. She shot me one last glare before I heard her footsteps thundering down the hallway and out the back door.

'Quick, into the study,' ordered Toby. 'Hugo, show us the way. We have to call for help.'

'Hey, you get back here, I haven't finished with you!' yelled Pegleg from the chair. 'I've gotta give you a thrashing, remember?'

Jasper flicked her plaits crossly as we filed out the door. 'I don't think you'll be doing anything for a while, do you?' she said sternly. 'Besides, thrashing's against the law.'

'Hello?' It seemed like ages before the person at the other end of the phone picked it up.

'Do you have a dog called Fabian?' I asked urgently. There was no time for niceties. Auntie Marge or Petronella could walk in the door at any moment and Pegleg was still bellowing threats from the next room.

There was a pause at the end of the phone. 'Who is this?' a man's voice said.

'My name is Hugo, and if you've lost a dog called Fabian I may be able to help you.'

Another pause. 'Fabian went missing four months ago . . . if this is a joke . . .'

Jasper, who was listening at the closed door of the study, started waving at me frantically. Somebody must be coming . . .

'It's not a joke, but listen carefully because I'm in a dangerous situation,' I said rapidly. 'Your dog was stolen by some people who live at ninety-five Yabbie Creek Road, Willowvale. Write that down. I don't know if he's still here or not.'

'How do I know you're telling the truth?'

'I've got Fabian's collar. It's brown leather with a silver name plate and a red registration tag, number 47389.'

Jasper was signalling frantically at me. I could hear footsteps coming down the hallway towards the study.

'Ninety-five Yabbie Creek Road, Willowvale,' I repeated. 'Get here as quickly as you can.' I hung up just as the door opened.

'Oh, it's only you, Flossie.' I breathed a huge sigh of relief. 'I thought it was Auntie Marge. Flossie, meet Frankie and Toby.'

Flossie smiled shyly as they shook hands. 'I feel like I already know you both. Hugo's told me so much about you and your newspaper.'

Jasper nervously opened the door a crack and peeked outside. 'It's okay — the coast's still clear.'

Flossie laughed. 'If you're worried about Petronella, don't be. I've locked her in my room and taken her keys.' She jangled the two bunches attached to her belt. 'As for Auntie Marge, the last time I saw her, she was chasing Scoop across a paddock. I think she'll be gone for a while.'

So once again, Flossie had helped us out of a tight spot. Tyson was right — she *was* like a guardian angel.

Only one thing worried me. Now that Flossie had

locked Petronella up, she had well and truly proved she was on our side. And that meant she'd be in big trouble with Auntie Marge and Pegleg after we escaped.

Flossie saw my concerned look and laughed again. 'At first I didn't want you to do anything that would close the camp down,' she explained. 'But after you told me about Pegleg being a criminal, I realised I couldn't stay here any longer. The next time you leave, Hugo — I'm coming with you.' A worried frown creased her forehead. 'I couldn't put out the bonfire, unfortunately. Petronella had stoked the collars up with a whole pile of dry wood.'

Toby waved his hand dismissively. He was sitting at the computer with Frankie. 'It doesn't matter. We've just found something much better — a floppy disk with details of every single dog Pegleg has ever stolen and sold.' He looked at us triumphantly. 'I knew he'd keep some sort of record!'

Things were happening so fast I could hardly keep up with them. We'd found some important new evidence to nail Pegleg with, and now Flossie was going to leave the camp with us. But at the back of my mind, I knew we couldn't sit around congratulating ourselves for too much longer. Pegleg Paddy was, after all, still in the next room — and Auntie Marge wouldn't be gone forever.

I picked up the phone and called the police.

It was Jasper who heard the sirens first.

'How many patrol cars did you call, Hugo?' she asked. 'Sounds like the entire cavalry's on their way here!'

I shrugged. 'Only one, as far as I know.'

Flossie walked over to a white plastic box mounted on the wall, and punched in some numbers. 'I'll open the gate for them.'

Frankie was at the window, watching the driveway. 'Ooh, here they come,' she squealed excitedly, as a police car with flashing blue lights and its siren blaring pulled up outside.

She turned around, wide-eyed. 'You'll never believe this, but there's *another* police car behind them!'

Jasper ran to the window. 'Unreal! And look — a third one's just turned up! With a taxi behind it! And another car! And — and — Toby, I think your dad's here too!'

We rushed outside. The driveway was so crowded it was like a shopping centre car park. There were sirens going and car doors slamming and people running all over the place. Frankie took a fresh film from her pocket, whipped it into her camera, and started taking pictures.

'What are you doing here, Dad?' asked Toby, as

Mr Trotter unfolded his long legs from the shiny blue Adventurer.

'We got a tip-off at the *Bugle*,' replied Mr Trotter, looking a bit bewildered. 'Saying the police were about to bust a crime-ring at the Fun Camp. I got out here as fast as I could to make sure you kids were safe.'

'Relax, Dad.' Toby patted his shoulder. 'It's all under control.'

A man I didn't recognise walked over to us. 'Are you Hugo? I'm Fabian's owner.' He looked around anxiously. 'Is Fabian here? Can I take him home with me?'

'You leave the details to us, sir.' A police woman in a smart blue suit interrupted him. 'Is this the boy who rang you? I'd like a word with you, son.'

'Hang about, I'm first,' said a tall young policeman firmly. 'Sergeant Standaloft from Willowvale Patrol. You're the boy who rang us, aren't you? Now what's all this about the Phantom Dog-nappers?'

Amidst all the chaos I hardly noticed the man and the woman who stepped out of the taxi, and stood quietly looking around them.

It was only when the woman called out 'Flora?' in a trembling voice that I looked up.

The woman had dark hair and a soft, sweet smile. The man had serious eyes and snow white hair.

I turned and saw Flossie, pale as a ghost and frozen like a statue on the front steps.

'Is it you?' she whispered uncertainly. 'Is it really you?'

And then she was running towards them, her long bare legs flying, and tears streaming down her face.

Chapter Ten

'We've got a problem,' Toby announced.

It was two days later and we were hard at work producing a special bumper edition of *Street Wise*. The Cave was like Central Station at peak hour: Frankie was running in and out with photographs as she developed them in her darkroom; Jasper and I were taking turns using the computer at home to write our stories then delivering them to Toby on disk; Scoop was following me like a shadow.

And as for Toby — well, our long-suffering editor was up to his eyeballs as he tried to get the newspaper finished by the deadline. That meant checking our stories for errors, putting snappy headlines on them, scanning photographs into Myron — then putting all the different pieces together like a jigsaw puzzle. Not to mention keeping track of the rest of us.

As luck would have it, we were all in the Cave to hear his announcement.

'We've got a problem,' he repeated, raising his voice to be heard above the noise.

I groaned. 'If this is a group problem, then include me out. I've got enough on my mind.' I pointed to Scoop. 'Mum and Dad get home tomorrow — and somehow, I've got to explain *him*!'

Toby grinned. 'No, this is a different sort of problem. A good one. We've just got too many excellent stories. I can't fit them all in the paper.'

He held up a proof — a practice run — of the front page. 'DOG-GONE IT!' screamed the headline. Underneath was a photograph of Auntie Marge and Pegleg Paddy being dragged away by Sergeant Standaloft and the other police. Auntie Marge looked really angry and Pegleg was shaking his fist at the camera. Then there was a headline in smaller writing under that, saying: 'Newspaper Kids Bust Illegal Puppy Factory'.

'That blank space is where I'll put your story, Hugo,' said Toby. 'It won't all fit on the front page, so I'll run the rest of it over on page two. What do you think?'

'Looks great,' I shrugged, still worried about Scoop. I kept hearing Dad's deep voice, booming *'No more strays!'*

'Brilliant headline, Toby,' added Jasper. 'That'll really get people's attention!'

'Well, the story's the important thing,' said Toby modestly. 'You just need a good headline to convince people to read it.'

I took the proof from him and started reading my story again.

> What a week! First, Jasper and I get sent to Auntie Marge's Fun Camp, which is in a spooky old horror house, for a holiday — the next thing we know, we're surrounded by hardened criminals. You see, Auntie Marge and her son Paddy were only running the Fun Camp as a cover for a stolen dog racket. Nobody suspected them because Auntie Marge used to be a champion dog breeder. Then she got kicked out by the other dog breeders for doing dishonest things. That's when she and Paddy came up with the idea of stealing dogs, and using kids like us to look after them . . .

Jasper ripped the page out of my hands.

'Where's *my* story?' She looked plaintively at Toby. 'Don't tell me Hugo's hogged the whole front page again. It's not fair!'

Toby picked up another proof. 'Here. Yours is the main story on page three. Don't forget — that's the next best thing. It's the first thing people see when they turn the front page.'

'Hmmmph!' Jasper looked miffed, but not for long. As soon as she saw her by-line — 'By Celebrity Reporter JASPER LILLEY' — she got a smug smile on her face like a cat that had just swallowed a canary.

'Who would have thought I'd find not just one celebrity, but *three* of them, at that horrible old Hell Camp?' she preened, waving the page triumphantly at me. 'I guess there's no substitute for sheer brilliance, huh?'

'ORPHAN GIRL FINDS MISSING PARENTS ON INTERNET,' said the headline. It seemed like everyone had forgotten that *I* was the one who found Flossie's parents. After all, I was the one who'd put their photographs on the Net, and sent them to every single university, hospital and safari park in Africa that was on-line. Trust Jasper to grab all the glory now that we were out of trouble. And she hadn't come up with a single suggestion about Scoop.

'Very clever,' I said grumpily, staring at the photograph of Flossie and her beaming parents in

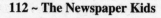

the article that Jasper had written.

They used to call her Flossie Fleabags the Orphan Girl. But thanks to a miracle on the Internet, Flora Hamilton has now been reunited with the parents she thought she'd lost forever.

'I still don't get it,' asked Frankie, from the depths of the old couch. 'How come her parents didn't come and get her?'

'Read the story,' ordered Jasper, being a pain. 'Everything you need to know is in my exclusive report.'

'They had a terrible accident in a safari park and both of them lost their memory,' I explained to Frankie, ignoring Jasper. 'They were in hospital all that time. The doctors and nurses . . .'

'. . . didn't know who they were or where to send them, until they saw their photographs on the Net,' interrupted Jasper breathlessly. 'As soon as the doctors mentioned Flora's name, Mr and Mrs Hamilton were cured. Their memory was instantly restored and they jumped on the next plane home.'

She flicked her plaits grandly. 'Now the *Blue Rock Bugle* wants to do a follow-up story on them. But I said, not until *Street Wise* comes out. After all, it is an exclusive. And I can't have my celebrities being hounded by reporters while they're still jet lagged.'

Toby and I looked at each other and rolled our eyes. The way Jasper was talking, you'd think she owned the Hamiltons — or, at the very least, adopted them.

'None of this solves our problem,' Toby reminded us impatiently. 'We've got all our regular features like Dr Death and the social pages, as well as the classified ads *and* all the reports about the puppy factory.' He grimaced. 'There's just not enough room for it all in one newspaper.'

'You can't drop any of them,' I said, alarmed. 'They're all too good. And don't forget my special report on what's happening to all the dogs now that Marge and Paddy are in jail.'

I knew that was one of the first questions people would ask, so I'd checked it out. And guess what? Most of the dogs had been returned to their owners. Silly old Aunt Marge. She thought she was being clever by telling Petronella to burn all the collars and destroy the evidence. But she forgot one important fact — silver doesn't burn. All the dogs' name tags were still intact, including their owners' phone numbers. The police found them among the ashes of Petronella's bonfire when they were looking for evidence. Most of the dogs had already been sold, of course — but thanks to the detailed computer data bank Toby had discovered, the police were able to find them all.

'Why don't we just make the paper bigger?' suggested Frankie. 'Then we wouldn't have to drop any stories at all. And,' she added slyly, 'you'll be able to run more of my photos.'

Toby blinked at us, considering the suggestion.

'I didn't think we'd be expanding this soon,' he said slowly. 'But I don't see any reason why not. The question is — can we keep filling the extra pages with really good stories?'

I looked at Jasper. She looked at me.

'I can if you can,' I said stiffly.

'Well, if you can, I *definitely* can!' retorted Jasper, tossing her head. 'In fact, I'm going to start right now. I've just had another brilliant thought — and I'd hate to waste it.'

I watched her flounce out of the Cave. One day, I thought hopefully, that head of hers will get so big, it'll pop . . .

'Scoop the Wonder Dog, hey?' Dad's voice was stern but his eyes twinkled as he put *Street Wise* down on the kitchen table. 'Not a bad story, Jasper. I'm amazed you could get so much detail out of an interview subject who can't actually talk.'

'You don't have to be human to be a celebrity,

Dad,' Jasper informed him. 'And after all, Scoop did save our lives. He was the real hero. If he hadn't run off with Paddy's wooden leg, who knows what might have happened.'

I looked at Jasper gratefully. For a big-headed, bossy older sister, she wasn't so bad sometimes.

Mum shuddered. 'When I think about those vile people . . .' She turned to Dad. 'As far as I'm concerned Nick, that little dog has earned his place in this house ten times over.'

Dad didn't say a word. He just kept turning the pages of *Street Wise* and frowning. It didn't look good.

Suddenly, he looked straight at me. 'My instincts are to say yes, Hugo.' My heart leapt. 'But there's one thing I'm concerned about.' My heart stopped mid-air, then did a great big belly flop back into my stomach.

'What's that?' I squeaked. Was he still mad about the mess on his shoes? Worried about Scoop barking? The cost of feeding him?

Dad cupped his chin in his hands and leaned forward. Mum, Jasper and I all leaned forward too, holding our breath and waiting for Dad to say something.

'Can he do any tricks, son?' Dad fixed me with a stern eye.

The question caught me by surprise.

'Tricks?' I said weakly. What was he going on about?

'Any dog worth his dinner has to be able to do at least one trick,' Dad said firmly. 'Proves he's got a few brains.'

A huge grin started to spread over my face. I ran to the kitchen door and whistled sharply. Two seconds later, Scoop barrelled through the door with a stick in his mouth and his tail wagging like a propellor.

In a daze, I took the stick out of his mouth. Then I threw it as far as I could. Mum, Dad, Jasper and I watched as it arced through the afternoon sunlight, and disappeared from view somewhere in the backyard.

'Go fetch!' I told Scoop. But he was already on his way.

The Newspaper Kids 1

★ Blue Rock Kid Power

by Juanita Phillips

Jasper nearly kills Toby on the skate ramp, then the Mayor decides to close the park. Everyone in Blue Rock is blaming the kids. Toby is the only person who knows the real story and it's a story that *must* be told! But making headlines and digging up secrets is a dangerous business. Someone doesn't want the newspaper to hit the streets and it looks like they'll do anything to stop it.

If a story breaks, the newspaper kids are on the case.

The Newspaper Kids 2

✱ Mandy Miami and the Miracle Motel

by Juanita Phillips

War has been declared!
Howard Fitzherbert has started his own
newspaper to try and run the newspaper kids
out of business! He's stealing all their ideas.
They need a special front page story. Toby's
favourite singer, Mandy Miami, could be
exactly what they want, but Mandy is so
mysterious, even her fan club don't know
how to find her. The World Wide Web holds
the clues but the newspaper kids aren't the
only ones surfing the Net – so is the Shark.

If a story breaks, the newspaper kids are
on the case!

The Newspaper Kids 4

Spooking Sally

by Juanita Phillips

Sally Champion is not afraid of anything!
She's not scared of ghosts or graveyards or
even Bonecrusher, the meanest dog in town.
So the newspaper kids have come up with the
biggest dare 'n' scare competition that Blue
Rock has ever seen – the *Street Wise*
Spooking Sally Challenge! The only problem
is, Sally really is hard to spook. But when
some rare dinosaur bones go missing, the
scene is set to scare Sally out of her skin!

If a story breaks, the newspaper kids are
on the case!